He Needed More Time With Her.

His mind filled with a vision of Alexa chasing his kids around, all wet from the tub. Warm memories pulled him in with a reminder of the family life he should be having right now and wasn't because of his workload. Having Alexa here felt so right.

It was right.

And so he wasn't sending her home in the morning. Not only did he need her help with the children, he wanted her to stay for personal reasons. The explosive chemistry they'd just discovered didn't come around often. Hell, he couldn't remember when he'd ever burned this much to have a particular woman. So much the craving filled his mind, as well as his body.

The extension of their trip presented the perfect opportunity to follow that attraction to its ultimate destination.

Landing her directly in his bed.

* * *

Dear Reader,

As an avid reader myself, I adore connected stories! When I'm intrigued by a secondary character in a novel, I'm ecstatic when that character gets his or her own happily-ever-after. It's especially a thrill when readers write to me, asking about a potential book for one of *my* characters.

In this case, readers have been asking for Seth Jansen's story since his extended family first appeared in one of my Silhouette Intimate Moments novels, *Explosive Alliance,* and then again in my early Silhouette Desire novels *Baby, I'm Yours* and *Under the Millionaire's Influence.* This book—*Billionaire's Jet Set Babies*—can be read as a stand-alone. However, if you would like to find those earlier reads about Seth and his family, they have all been reissued in ebook form. And the two Silhouette Desire novels are being re-released in print form in November 2011 as a 2-in-1 for Harlequin Showcase.

Thanks again to all of you who sent shout-outs for Seth Jansen's story. I had a blast penning the long-awaited happily-ever-after for this jet-setting hero!

Cheers,

Catherine Mann

www.CatherineMann.com

CATHERINE MANN

BILLIONAIRE'S JET SET BABIES

Recycling programs
for this product may
not exist in your area.

ISBN-13: 978-0-373-73128-2

BILLIONAIRE'S JET SET BABIES

Copyright © 2011 by Catherine Mann

This edition published by arrangement with Harlequin Books S.A.

For questions and comments about the quality of this book please contact us
at Customer_eCare@Harlequin.ca.

® and TM are trademarks of Harlequin Books S.A., used under license.
Trademarks indicated with ® are registered in the United States Patent
and Trademark Office, the Canadian Trade Marks Office and in other
countries.

www.Harlequin.com

Printed in U.S.A.

Books by Catherine Mann

Harlequin Desire

Acquired: The CEO's Small-Town Bride #2090
Billionaire's Jet Set Babies #2115

Silhouette Desire

Baby, I'm Yours #1721
Under the Millionaire's Influence #1787
The Executive's Surprise Baby #1837
†*Rich Man's Fake Fiancée* #1878
†*His Expectant Ex* #1895
Propositioned Into a Foreign Affair #1941
†*Millionaire in Command* #1969
Bossman's Baby Scandal #1988
†*The Tycoon Takes a Wife* #2013
Winning It All #2031
    "Pregnant with the Playboy's Baby"
*The Maverick Prince #2047
*His Thirty-Day Fiancée #2061
*His Heir, Her Honor #2071

†The Landis Brothers
*Rich, Rugged & Royal

All backlist available in ebook

CATHERINE MANN

USA TODAY bestselling author Catherine Mann is living out her own fairy-tale ending on a sunny Florida beach with her Prince Charming husband and their four children. With more than thirty-five books in print in more than twenty countries, she has also celebrated wins for both a RITA® Award and a Booksellers' Best Award. Catherine enjoys chatting with readers online—thanks to the wonders of the wireless internet, which allows her to network with her laptop by the water! To learn more about her work, visit her website, www.catherinemann.com, or reach her by snail mail at P.O. Box 6065, Navarre, FL 32566.

To Amelia Richard: a treasured reader,
reviewer and friend. Thank you for all you've done to
help spread the word about my stories. You're awesome!

One

Alexa Randall had accumulated an eclectic boxful of lost and found items since opening her own cleaning company for charter jets. There were the standard smart phones, portfolios, tablets, even a Patek Philippe watch. She'd returned each to its owner.

Then there were the stray panties and men's boxers, even the occasional sex toys from Mile High Club members. All of those items, she'd picked up with latex gloves and tossed in the trash.

But today marked a first find ever in the history of A-1 Aircraft Cleaning Services. Never before had she found a baby left on board—actually, *two* babies.

Her bucket of supplies dropped to the industrial blue carpet with a heavy thud that startled the sleeping pair. Yep, two infants, apparently twins with similar blond curly hair and cherub cheeks. About one year old, perhaps? A boy and a girl, it seemed, gauging from their pink and blue smocked outfits and gender-matched car seats.

Tasked to clean the jet alone, Alexa had no one to share her shock with. She flipped on another table lamp in the main compartment of the sleek private jet, the lighting in the hangar sketchy at best even at three in the afternoon.

Both kids were strapped into car seats resting on the leather sofa along the side of the plane, which was Seth Jansen's personal aircraft. As in *the* Seth Jansen of Jansen Jets. The self-made billionaire who'd raked in a fortune inventing some must-have security device for airports to help combat possible terrorist attacks on planes during takeoffs and landings. She admired the man's entrepreneurial spirit.

Landing his account would be her company's big break. She needed this first cleaning of his aircraft to go off without a hitch.

Tiny fists waved for a second, slowing, lowering, until both babies began to settle back to sleep. Another huffy sigh shuddered through the girl before her breaths evened out. Her little arm landed on a piece of paper safety-pinned to the girl's hem.

Narrowing her eyes, Alexa leaned forward and read:

Seth,
You always say you want more time with the twins, so here's your chance. Sorry for the short notice, but a friend surprised me with a two-week spa retreat. Enjoy your "daddy time" with Olivia and Owen!
XOXO,
Pippa

Pippa?

Alexa straightened again, horrified. Really? Really!

Pippa Jansen, as in the *ex*-Mrs. Jansen, had dumped off her infants on their father's jet. Unreal. Alexa stuffed her fists into the pockets of her navy chinos, standard uniform for A-1 cleaning staff along with a blue polo shirt bearing the company's logo.

And who signed a note to their obviously estranged baby daddy with kisses and hugs? Alexa sank down into a fat chair across from the pint-size passengers. Bigger question of the day, who left babies unattended on an airplane?

A crappy parent, that's who.

The rich and spoiled rotten, who played by their own rules, a sad reality she knew only too well from growing up in that world. People had told her how lucky she was as a kid—lucky to have a dedicated nanny that she spent more time with than she did with either of her parents.

The best thing that had ever happened to her? Her father bankrupted the family's sportswear chain— once worth billions, now worth zip. That left Alexa the recipient of a trust fund from Grandma containing a couple of thousand dollars.

She'd used the money to buy a partnership in a cleaning service about to go under because the aging owner could no longer carry the workload on her own. Bethany—her new partner—had been grateful for Alexa's energy and the second chance for A-1 Aircraft Cleaning Services to stay afloat. Using Alexa's contacts from her family's world of luxury and extravagance she had revitalized the struggling business. Alexa's ex-husband, Travis, had been appalled by her new occupation and offered to help out financially so she wouldn't have to work.

She would rather scrub toilets.

And the toilet on this particular Gulfstream III jet was very important to her. She had to land the Jansen Jet contract and hopefully this one-time stint would impress him enough to cinch the deal. Her business needed this account to survive, especially in today's tough economy. If she failed, she could lose everything and A-1 might well face Chapter 11 bankruptcy. She'd hardly believed her luck when she'd been asked by another cleaning company to subcontract out on one of the Jansen Jets—this jet.

Now that she'd found these two babies, she was screwed. She swept particles of sand from the seat into her hand, eyed the fingerprints on the windows, could almost feel the grit rising from the carpet fiber. But she couldn't just clean up, restock the Evian water and pretend these kids weren't here. She needed to contact airport security, which was going to land Jansen's ex-wife in hot water, possibly him as well. That would piss off Jansen. And the jet still wouldn't be serviced. And then he would never consider her for the contract.

Frustration and a hefty dose of anger stung stronger than a bucket full of ammonia. Scratch cleaning detail for now, scratch cinching this deal that would finally take her company out of the red. She had to locate the twins' father ASAP.

Alexa unclipped the cell phone from her waist and thumbed her directory to find the number for Jansen Jets, which she happened to have since she'd been trying to get through to the guy for a month. She'd never made it further than his secretary, who'd agreed to pass along Alexa's business prospectus.

She eyed the sleeping babies. Maybe some good could come from this mess after all.

Today, she would finally have the chance to talk to the boss, just not how she'd planned and not in a way that would put him in a receptive mood...

The phone stopped ringing as someone picked up.

"Jansen Jets, please hold." As quickly as the thick female Southern drawl answered, the line clicked and Muzak filled the air waves with soulless contemporary tunes.

A squawk from one of the car seats drew her attention. She looked up fast to see Olivia wriggling in her seat, kicking free a Winnie the Pooh blanket. The little girl spit out her Piglet pacifier and whimpered, getting louder until her brother scrunched up his face, blinking awake and none too happy. His Eeyore pacifier dangled from a clip attached to his blue sailor outfit.

Two pairs of periwinkle-blue eyes stared at her, button noses crinkled. Owen's eyes filled with tears. Olivia's bottom lip thrust outward again.

Tucking the Muzak-humming phone under her chin, Alexa hefted the iconic Burberry plaid diaper bag off the floor.

"Hey there, little ones," she said in what she hoped was a conciliatory tone. She'd spent so little time around babies she could only hope she pegged it right. "I know, I know, sweetie, I'm a stranger, but I'm all you've got right now."

And how crummy was that? She stifled another spurt of anger at the faceless Pippa who'd dropped her children off like luggage. When had the spa-hopping mama expected their father to locate them?

"I'm assuming you're Olivia." Alexa tickled the bare foot of the girl wearing a pink smocked dress.

Olivia giggled, and Alexa pulled the pink lace bootie from the baby's mouth. Olivia thrust out her bottom lip—until Alexa unhooked a teething ring from the diaper bag and passed it over to the chubby-cheeked girl.

"And you must be Owen." She tweaked his blue tennis shoe—still on his foot as opposed to his sister who was ditching her other booty across the aisle with the arm of a major league pitcher. "Any idea where your daddy is? Or how much longer he'll be?"

She'd been told by security she had about a half hour to service the inside of the jet in order to be out before Mr. Jansen arrived. As much as she would have liked to meet him, it was considered poor form for the cleaning staff to still be on hand. She'd expected her work and a business card left on the silver drink tray to speak for itself.

So much for her well laid plans.

She scooped up a baby blanket from the floor, folded it neatly and placed it on the couch. She smoothed back Owen's sweaty curls. Going quiet, he stared back at her just as the on hold Muzak cued up "Sweet Caroline"— the fourth song so far. Apparently she'd been relegated to call waiting purgatory.

How long until the kids got hungry? She peeked into the diaper bag for supplies. Maybe she would luck out and find more contact info along the way. Sippy cups of juice, powdered formula, jars of food and diapers, diapers, diapers...

The clank of feet on the stairway outside yanked her upright. She dropped the diaper bag and spun around fast, just as a man filled the open hatch. A tall and broad-shouldered man.

He stood with the sun backlighting him, casting his face in mysterious shadows.

Alexa stepped in front of the babies instinctively, protectively. "Good afternoon. What can I do for you?"

Silently he stepped deeper into the craft until overhead lights splashed over his face and she recognized him from her internet searches. Seth Jansen, founder and CEO of Jansen Jets.

Relief made her knees wobbly. She'd been saved from a tough decision by Jansen's early arrival. And, wow, did the guy ever know how to make an entrance.

From press shots she'd seen he was good-looking, with a kind of matured Abercrombie & Fitch beach hunk appeal. But no amount of Google Images could capture the impact of this tremendously attractive self-made billionaire in person.

Six foot three or four, he filled the charter jet with raw muscled *man*. He wasn't some pale pencil pusher. He was more the size of a keen-eyed lumberjack, in a suit. An expensive, tailored suit.

The previously spacious cabin now felt tight. Intimate.

His sandy-colored hair—thick without being shaggy—sported sun-kissed streaks of lighter blond, the kind that came naturally from being outside rather than sitting in a salon chair. His tan and toned body gave further testimony to that. No raccoon rings around the eyes from tanning bed glasses. The scent of crisp air clung to him, so different from the boardroom aftershaves of her father and her ex. She scrunched her nose at even the memory of cloying cologne and cigars.

Even his eyes spoke of the outdoors. They were the same vibrant green she'd once seen in the waters off the Caribbean coast of St. Maarten, the sort of sparkling green that made you want to dive right into their cool depths. She turned shivery all over just thinking about taking a swim in those pristine waters.

She seriously needed to lighten up on the cleaning supply fumes. How unprofessional to stand here and gawk like a sex-starved divorcée—which she was.

"Good afternoon, Mr. Jansen. I'm Alexa Randall with A-1 Aircraft Cleaning Services."

He shrugged out of his suit jacket, gray pinstripe and almost certainly an Ermenegildo Zegna, a brand known for its no-nonsense look. Expensive. Not surprising.

His open shirt collar, with his burgundy tie loosened did surprise her, however. Overall, she got the impression of an Olympic swimmer confined in an Italian suit.

"Right." He checked his watch—the only non-*GQ* item on him. He wore what appeared to be a top-of-the-line diver's timepiece. "I'm early, I know, but I need to leave right away so if you could speed this up, I would appreciate it."

Jansen charged by, not even hesitating as he passed the two tykes. *His* tykes.

She cleared her throat. "You have a welcoming crew waiting for you."

"I'm sure you're mistaken." He stowed his briefcase, his words clipped. "I'm flying solo today."

She held up Pippa's letter. "It appears, Mr. Jansen, your flight plans have changed."

Seth Jansen stopped dead in his tracks. He looked back over his shoulder at Alexa Randall, the owner of a new, small company that had been trying to get his attention for at least a month. Yeah, he knew who the drop-dead gorgeous blonde was. But he didn't have time to listen to her make a pitch he already knew would be rejected.

While he appreciated persistence as a business professional himself, he did not like gimmicks. "Let's move along to the point, please."

He had less than twenty minutes to get his Gulfstream III into the air and on its way from Charleston, South Carolina, to St. Augustine, Florida. He had a business meeting he'd been working his ass off to land for six months—dinner with the head of security for the Medinas, a deposed royal family that lived in exile in the United States.

Big-time account.

Once in a lifetime opportunity.

And the freedom to devote more of his energies to the philanthropic branch of this company. Freedom. It had a different meaning these days than when he'd flown crop dusters to make his rent back, in North Dakota.

"This—" she waved a piece of floral paper in front of him "—is the point."

As she passed over the slip of paper, she stepped aside and revealed—holy crap—his kids. He looked down at the letter fast.

Two lines into the note, his temple throbbed. What the hell was Pippa thinking, leaving the twins this way?

How long had they been in here? And why had she left him a damn note, for Pete's sake?

He pulled out his cell phone to call his ex. Her voice mail picked up immediately. She was avoiding him, no doubt.

A text from Pippa popped up in his in-box. He opened the message and it simply read, Want 2 make sure you know. Twins r waiting for you at plane. Sorry 4 short notice. XOXO.

"What the h—?" He stopped himself short before he cursed in front of his toddlers who were just beginning to form words. He tucked his phone away and faced Alexa Randall. "I'm sorry my ex added babysitter duties to your job today. Of course I'll pay you extra. Did you happen to notice which way Pippa headed out?"

Because he had some choice words for her when he found her.

"Your ex-wife wasn't here when I arrived." Alexa held up her own cell phone, her thumb swiping away a print. "I tried to contact your office, but your assistant wouldn't let me get a word out before shifting me over to Muzak. It's looped twice while I waited. Much longer and I would have had to call security, which would have brought in child services—"

He held up a hand, sick to his gut already. "Thanks. I get the picture. I owe you for cleaning up after my ex-wife's recklessness as well."

His blood pressure spiked higher until he saw red. Pippa had left the children unattended in an airplane at his privately owned airport? What had his security people been thinking, letting Pippa just wander around the aircraft that way? These were supposed to be the days of increased precautions and safety measures, and yet they must have assumed because she was his ex-wife that garnered her a free pass around the facility. Not so.

Heads were going to roll hard and fast over this. No one put the safety of his children at risk.

No one.

He crumpled the note in his fist and pitched it aside. Forcing his face to smooth so he wouldn't scare the babies, he unstrapped the buckle on his daughter's car seat.

"Hey there, princess." He held Olivia up high and thought about how she'd squealed with delight over the baby swing on the sprawling oak in his backyard. "Did you have fruit for lunch?"

She grinned, and he saw a new front tooth had come in on top. She smelled like peaches and baby shampoo and there weren't enough hours in the day to take in all the changes happening too quickly.

He loved his kids more than anything, had since the second he'd seen their fists waving in an ultrasound. He'd been damn lucky Pippa let him be there when they were born, considering she'd already started divorce proceedings at that point. He hated not being with them every day, hated missing even one milestone. But the timing for this visit couldn't be worse.

Seth tucked Olivia against his chest and reached to ruffle his son's hair. "Hey, buddy. Missed you this week."

Owen stuck out his tongue and offered up his best raspberry.

The petite blonde dressed in trim, pressed chinos popped a pacifier into Owen's mouth then knelt to pick up the crumpled note and pitch it into her cleaning bucket. "I assume today isn't your scheduled visitation."

She would be right on that. Although why the disdain in her voice? Nobody—single parent or not—would appreciate having their kids dumped off in their workplace. Not to mention he was mad as hell at Pippa for just dropping them off unannounced.

What if someone else had boarded this plane?

Thank God, this woman—Alexa—had been the one to find them. He knew who she was, but Pippa hadn't known jack when she'd unloaded his children.

Of all the reckless, irresponsible…

Deep breath. He unbuckled Owen as well and scooped him up, too, with an ease he'd learned from walking the floors with them when they were infants. Just as he'd needed calm then, he forced it through his veins now.

Getting pissed off wouldn't accomplish anything. He had to figure out what to do with his children when he was scheduled to fly out for a meeting with multimillion dollar possibilities.

When he'd first moved to South Carolina, he'd been a dumb ass, led by glitz. That's how he'd ended up married to his ex. He'd grown up with more spartan, farm values that he'd somehow lost in his quest for beaches and billions.

Now, he itched inside his high-priced starched shirt and longed for the solitude of those flights. But he had long ago learned if he wanted to do business with certain people, he had to dress the part and endure the stuffy business meetings. And he very much wanted to do business with the Medina family based out of Florida. He glanced at his watch and flinched. Damn it. He needed to be in the air already, on his way to St. Augustine. At the moment, he didn't have time for a sandwich, much less to find a qualified babysitter.

He would just have to make time. "Could you hold Owen for a second while I make some calls?"

"Sure, no problem." Alexa stopped straightening his jacket on the hanger and extended her arms.

As he passed his son over, Seth's hand grazed her breast. Her very soft, tempting breast. Just that fast touch pumped pure lust through his overworked body. It was more than just "nice, a female" kind of notice. His body was going on alert, saying "I will make it my mission in life to undress you."

She gasped lightly, not in outrage but more like someone who'd been zapped with some static. For him, it was more like a jolt from a light socket.

Olivia rested her head on his shoulder with a sleepy sigh, bringing him back to reality. He was a father with responsibilities.

Still, he was a man. Why hadn't he noticed the power of the pull to this woman when he'd walked onto the plane? Had he grown so accustomed to wealth that he'd stopped noticing "the help"? That notion didn't sit well with him at all.

But it also didn't keep him from looking at Alexa more closely.

Her pale blond hair was pulled back in a simple silver clasp. Navy chino pants and a light blue shirt— the company uniform—matched her eyes. It also fit her loosely, but not so much that it hid her curves.

Before the kids, before Pippa, he would have asked Alexa for her number, made plans to take her out on a riverboat dinner cruise where he would kiss her senseless under a starry sky. But these days he didn't have time for dating. He worked and when he wasn't on the job he saw his kids.

With a stab of regret, his gaze raked back over her T-shirt with the A-1 Aircraft Cleaning logo. He'd seen that same emblem in the cover letter she'd sent with her prospectus.

He also recalled why he hadn't gotten any further than the cover letter and the fledgling business's flyer—where he'd seen her headshot.

Following his eyes, she looked down at her shirt and met his gaze dead-on. "Yes, I have a proposal on your desk." Alexa cocked one eyebrow. "I assume that's why you were looking at my shirt?"

"Of course, why else?" he answered dryly. "You should have received an answer from my secretary."

"I did, and when you're not in a hurry—" she smoothed back her already immaculate hair "—I would appreciate the opportunity to explore your reasons for rejecting my initial bid."

"I'll save us both some time. I'm not interested in the lowest bidder or taking a risk on such a small company."

Her sky-blue eyes narrowed perceptively. "You didn't read my proposal all the way through, did you?"

"I read until my gut told me to stop." He didn't have time to waste on page after page of something he already knew wasn't going to work.

"And you're saying that your gut spoke up quickly."

"Afraid so," he said shortly, hoping to end an awkward situation with his best boardroom bite. A suspicion niggled. "Why is it you're here cleaning today instead of someone from my regular company?"

"They subcontracted A-1 when they overbooked.

Obviously I wasn't going to turn down the opportunity to impress you." She stood tall and undaunted in spite of his rejection.

Spunky and hot. Dangerous combo.

He fished his phone from his suit coat again. "I really do need to start making some calls."

"Don't let me keep you." She dipped her hand into the diaper bag and pulled out two rice cakes. She passed one to Owen and the other to Olivia. All the while Owen tugged at her hair, watching the way the white-blond strands glittered in the light. "That should keep them quiet while you talk."

Interesting that Alexa never once winced, even when Owen's fingers tangled and tugged. Not that he could blame his son in the least.

Seth thumbed the numbers on his phone and started with placing a call to his ex-wife—that again went straight to voice mail. Damn it. He then moved on to dialing family members.

Five frustrating conversations later, he'd come up empty on all counts. Either his kids were hellions and no one wanted to watch them, or he was having a serious run of bad luck.

Although their excuses were rock solid. His cousin Paige was on lockdown since her two daughters had strep throat. His cousin Vic had announced his wife was in labor with child number three—which meant *her* sisters were watching her other two kids, in addition to their own. But damn it, he'd needed to take off five minutes ago.

Brooding, he watched Alexa jostle Owen on her shapely hip. She was obviously a natural with kids. She wasn't easily intimidated, important when dealing with his strong-willed offspring. She'd protected the kids when she found them alone on the plane. He'd seen proof of her determination and work ethic. An idea formed in his head, and as much as he questioned the wisdom of it, the notion still took root.

In spite of what he'd told her, he had read more of her proposal than the cover letter, enough to know something about her. He was interested in her entrepreneurial spirit—she'd done a solid job revitalizing a company that had virtually been on financial life support. Still, his gut told him he couldn't afford to take a risk on this part of his business, especially not now. Now that he was expanding, he needed to hire a larger, more established cleaning chain, even if it cost him extra.

But he needed a nanny and she'd passed the high-level background check needed to work in an airport. Her life had been investigated more thoroughly than anyone he would get from a babysitting service. Not to mention a babysitting service would send over a total stranger that his kids might hate. At least he'd met this woman, had access to her life story. Most importantly, he saw her natural rapport with the twins. He would be nearby in the hotel at all times—even during meetings—if she had questions about their routine.

She was actually a godsend.

Decision made, he forged ahead. "While I don't think your company's the right one to service Jansen Jets, *I* have a proposal for *you*."

"I'm not sure I understand?"

"You fly with me and the kids to St. Augustine, be Owen and Olivia's nanny for the next twenty-four hours and I'll let you verbally pitch your agency's proposal to me again, in detail." The more he spelled it out, the better the idea sounded. "I'll give you a few pointers about why my gut spoke up so quickly in case you want to make adjustments for future proposals to other companies. I'll even pass along your name to possible contacts, damn good contacts. And of course you'll be paid, a week's worth of wages for one day's work."

Was he taking advantage here? He didn't think so. He was offering her a business "in" she wouldn't have otherwise. If her verbal proposal held together, he would mention her business to some of his connections. And yes, give her those tips to help cinch a deal elsewhere. She would land jobs, just not his.

She eyed him suspiciously. "Twenty-four hours of Mary Poppins duty in exchange for a critique and some new contacts?"

"That should be long enough for me to make alternative arrangements." There'd been a time when twenty-four hours with a woman would be more than enough time to seduce her as well. His eyes roved over Alexa's curves once more, regretting that he wouldn't be able to brush up on those skills during this trip.

"And you trust me, a stranger, with your children?" Disdain dripped from her voice.

"Do you think this is the right time to call me a crummy father?" Though he had to appreciate her protective instincts when it came to his children.

"You could just ring up a nanny service."

"Already thought of that. They wouldn't get here in time and my kids might not like the person they send. Olivia and Owen have taken to you." Unable to resist, he tapped the logo just above her breast. Lightly. Briefly. His finger damn near shot out a flame like a Bic lighter. "And I do know who you are. I read enough of your proposal to learn you've passed your security check for airport work."

"Well, tomorrow is usually my day off…" She dusted the logo on her shirt, as if his touch lingered. "You'll really listen to my pitch and give me tips, mention my company to others?"

"Scout's honor." He smiled for the first time all day, seeing victory in sight.

"I want you to know I'm not giving up on persuading you to sign me up for Jansen Jets as well."

"Fair enough. You're welcome to try."

She eyed both the children then looked back to him. He knew when he'd presented an irresistible proposition. Now he just needed to wait for her to see this was a win-win situation.

Although he needed for her to realize that quickly. "I have about two minutes left here," he pressed. "If your answer's no, get to it so I can make use of the rest of my time to secure alternative arrangements." Although God only knew what those might be.

"Okay." She nodded in agreement although her furrowed brow broadcast a hefty dose of reservation. "You have yourself a deal. I'll call my partner to let her know so she can cover—"

"Great," he interrupted. "But do it while you buckle up the kids and yourself. We're out of here." He settled Olivia back into her car seat with a quick kiss on her forehead.

Alexa looked up quickly from fastening Owen into his safety seat. "Where's the pilot?"

He stared into her pale blue eyes and imagined them shifting colors as he made her as hot for him as he was for her. God, it would be damn tough to have this jaw-dropping female working beside him for the next twenty-four hours. But his children were his top priority.

So he simply smiled—and, yes, took a hefty dose of pleasure in seeing her pupils widen with awareness. "The pilot? That would be me."

with his empty hands still raised... or try to stay silent, or
break free and make a dash for the punishing surf of the
ocean.

He stopped short and stared, rage still at a boil. But
a glimmer of humor lurking within stirred shiftily, threatening
him... he didn't like it one bit.

Two

Her stomach dropped and she prayed the Gulfstream III wouldn't do the same in Seth Jansen's hands.

Turning off her cell after deleting four missed calls
from her mother and leaving a message for her partner,
Bethany, Alexa double-checked the safety belts for both
children and buckled her own. Watching Seth slide into
the pilot's seat, she reminded herself he owned a charter
jet company so of course it made sense he could pilot
a plane himself. She'd flown on private aircraft during
her entire childhood, trusting plenty of aviators she'd
never even met to get her safely from point A to point B.
So why was she so nervous with this guy at the helm?

Because he'd thrown her off balance.

Boarding the plane earlier, she'd had such optimism,
a solid approach in place and control of her world. In the

span of less than ten minutes, Seth Jansen had seized control of not just the plane, but her carefully made plan.

The kind of bargain he'd proposed was so unexpected, outrageous even. But too good an opportunity to pass up. She needed to take a deep breath, relax and focus on learning everything she could about him, to give her an edge in negotiations.

Even knowing he must have his pilot's license, she wouldn't have expected someone as wealthy as him willing to fly himself. She'd thought he would have someone else "chauffeuring" while he banged back a few drinks or took a nap. Like her dad would have done during their annual family vacation, a one-week trip that was supposed to make up for all the time they never spent together during the year.

Not that she saw much of either of her parents even then. While on vacation, the nanny had taken her to amusement parks or sightseeing or to the slopes while her father attended to "emergency" business and her mother went to the spa.

Simmering over old memories, Alexa polished the metal seatbelt buckle absently with the hem of her shirt as she watched Seth Jansen complete his preflight routine.

The door to the cockpit had been left open. Seth adjusted the mic on the headset, his mouth moving, although she couldn't hear him as the engines hummed to life. Smooth as silk, the plane left the hangar, past a row of parked smaller aircraft until he taxied to the end of the runway and stopped.

Nerves pattered up from her stomach to the roots of her hair. The jet engines roared louder, louder still, and yet she could swear she heard Seth's deep voice calmly blending with the aerial symphony.

Words drifted back...

"Charleston tower... Gulfstream alpha, two, one, prepared... Roger... Ready for takeoff..."

The luxury craft eased forward again, Seth's hands steady on the yoke and power. Confidence radiated from his every move, so much so she found herself relaxing into the butter-soft leather sofa. Her hands fell to rest on the handle of each car seat, claiming her charges. Her babies, for the next twenty-four hours.

Her heart squeezed with old regrets. Her marriage to Travis had been an unquestionable failure. While part of her was relieved there hadn't been children hurt by their breakup, another part of her grieved for the babies that might have been.

The nose of the plane lifted as the aircraft swooped upward. Olivia and Owen squirmed in their seats. Alexa reached for the diaper bag, panic stirring. Did they want a bottle? A toy? And if they needed a diaper change there wasn't a thing she could do about that for a while. Just when the panic started to squeeze her chest, the noise of the engines and the pacifiers she'd used to help their ears soothed them back into their unfinished nap.

The diaper bag slid from her grip, thudding on the floor. Relaxing, she stared across the aisle out the window as they left Charleston behind. She also left behind an empty apartment and a silent phone since her married friends had dropped away after her divorce.

Church steeples and spires dotted the ocean-locked landscape. So many, the historic town had earned nicknames of the Holy City and the City by the Sea. After their financial meltdown, her parents had relocated to a condo in Boca Raton to start over—away from the gossip.

How ironic that her parents' initial reservations about Travis had been so very far off base. They'd begged him to sign a prenuptial agreement. She'd told them to take their prenup and go to hell. Travis had insisted he didn't care and signed the papers anyway. She thought she'd found her dream man, finally someone who would love her for herself.

Not that the contract had mattered in the end since her father had blown through the whole fortune anyway. By the time they'd broken up, her ex hadn't wanted anything to do with her, her messy family dysfunction, or what he called her germaphobic ways.

The way Travis had simply fallen out of love with her had kicked the hell out of her self-esteem there for a while. She couldn't even blame the breakup on another woman. No way in hell was she going to let a man have control of her heart or her life ever again.

All the more reason she had to make a go of her cleaning business and establish her independence. She had no other marketable skills, apart from a host of bills and a life to rebuild in her beloved hometown.

So here she was, on a plane bound for St. Augustine with a stranger and two heart-tuggingly adorable babies. The coastline looked miniscule now outside the window as they reached their cruising altitude.

"Hey, Alexa?"

Seth's voice pulled her attention away from the view. He stood in the archway between the cockpit and the seating area.

Her stomach jolted again. "Shouldn't you be flying the plane?"

"It's on autopilot for the moment. Since the kids are sleeping, I want you to come up front. The flight isn't long, but it will give us the chance to talk through some specifics about your time with the twins."

She saw the flinty edge of calculation in his jewel-toned eyes. He may have offered her a deal back at the airport, but now he intended to interview her further before he turned over his children to her. A flicker of admiration lit through the disdain she had felt for him earlier.

Giving each baby another quick check and finding them snoozing away, binkies half in, half out of their slack mouths, she unbuckled, reassured she could safely leave them for a few minutes. She walked the short distance to Seth and stopped in the archway, waiting for him to move back to the pilot's seat.

Still, he stood immobile and aloof, other than those glinting green eyes that swept over her face. The crisp scent of him rode the recycled air to tempt her nose, swirling deeper inside her with each breath. Her breasts tingled with awareness, her body overcome with the urge to lean into him, press the aching fullness of her chest against the hard wall of manly muscles.

She shivered. He smiled arrogantly as if completely cognizant of just how much he affected her on a physical level. Seth stepped back brusquely, returning to the pilot's spot on the left and waving her into the copilot's seat on the right.

Strapping in, she stared at the gauges around her, the yoke moving automatically in front of her. Seth tapped buttons along the control panel and resumed flying the plane. Still, the steering in front of her mirrored his movements until she felt connected to him in some mystical manner.

She resented the way he sent her hormones into overdrive with just the sound of his husky voice or the intensity of his sharp gaze. She was here to do a job, damn it, not bring a man into her already too complicated life.

Twisting her fingers together in her lap, she forced her thoughts back to their jobs. "What's so important about this particular meeting that it can't be rescheduled?"

"I have small mouths to feed. Responsibilities." He stayed steadily busy as he talked, his eyes roving the gauges, his hands adjusting the yoke. "Surely you understand that, and if not, then I don't even need to read your proposal." He winked.

"Thank you for the Business 101 lecture, Mr. Jansen." She brushed specks of dust from a gauge. "I was really just trying to make conversation, but if you're more comfortable hanging out here alone, I'll be glad to return to the back."

"Sorry... And call me Seth," he said with what sounded like genuine contrition. "Long day. Too many surprises."

She glanced back at the sleeping babies, suddenly realizing they had miniature versions of his strong chin. "I can see that. What do you do to relax?"

"Fly."

He stared out at the expanse of blue sky and puffy clouds, and she couldn't miss the buzz radiating from him. Jansen Jets wasn't just a company to him. He'd turned his hobby, his true love, into a financial success. Not many could accomplish such a feat. Maybe she could learn something about business from him after all.

"You were looking forward to this time in the air, weren't you? What should have been your relaxing hour for the day has become a stressor."

"I've gotta ask..." He looked over at her quickly, brow furrowed. "Is the psychoanalysis included in the cleanup fee?"

She winced as his words hit a little too close to a truth of her own. Travis used to complain about that same trait. Well, she did have plenty of practice in what a shrink would say after all the time she'd spent in analysis as a teenager. The whole point had been to internalize those healthier ways of thinking. She'd needed the help, no question, but she'd also needed her parents. When they hadn't heard her, she'd started crying out for their attention in other ways, ways that had almost cost her life.

Her thoughts were definitely getting too deep and dark, and therefore too distracting. Something about this man and his children made her visit places in her mind she normally kept closed off. "Like I said, just making small talk. I thought you wanted me to come up here for conversation, to dig a little deeper into the background of your new, temporary nanny. If you don't want to chat, simply say so."

"You're right. I do. And the first thing I've learned is that you don't back down, which is a very good thing. It takes a strong person to stand up to the twins when they're in a bad mood." He shuddered melodramatically, his complaint totally undercut by the pride in his voice. Mr. Button-Up Businessman loosened up a little when he spoke of his kids. "What made you trade in your white gloves at tea for white glove cleaning?"

So he knew a little about her privileged upbringing as well. "You did more than just read my cover letter."

"I recognized your name—or rather your return to your maiden name. Your father was once a client of a competing company. Your husband chartered one of my planes."

"My ex-husband," she snapped.

He nodded, his fingers whitening as his grip tightened on the yoke. "So, back to my original question. What made you reach for the vacuum cleaner?"

"Comes with the business."

"Why choose this particular line of work?"

Because she didn't have a super cool hobby like he did? She'd suffered a rude awakening after her divorce was finalized a year ago, and she realized she had no money and no marketable skills.

Her one negligible talent? Being a neat-freak with a need to control her environment. Pair that with insights into the lifestyles of the rich and spoiled and she'd fashioned a career. But that answer sounded too half-baked and not particularly professional.

"Because I understand the needs of the customer, beyond just a clean space, I know the unique services that make the job stand out." True enough, and since he seemed to be listening, she continued, "Keeping records of allergies, favored scents, personal preferences for the drink bar can make the difference between a successful flight and a disaster. Flying in a charter jet isn't simply an air taxi service. It's a luxury experience and should be treated as such."

"You understand the world since you lived in it."

Lived. Past tense. "I want to be successful on my own merits rather than mooch off the family coffers."

Or at least she liked to think she would have felt that way if there had been any lucre left in the Randall portfolio.

"Why work in this particular realm, the aircraft world?" He gestured around the jet with a broad hand.

Her eyes snagged on the sprinkling of fair hair along his forearm. Tanned skin contrasted with the white cuffs of his rolled up sleeves and wow did her fingertips ever itch to touch him. To see if his bronzed-god flesh still carried the warmth of the sun.

It had been so long since she'd felt these urges. Her divorce had left her emotionally gutted. She'd tried dating a couple of times, but the chemistry hadn't been there. Her new business venture consumed her. Or rather, it had until right now, when it mattered most.

"I'm missing your point." No surprise since she was staring at his arm like an idiot.

"You're a...what...history major?"

"Art history, and being that close means you read my bio. You do know a lot more about me than you let on at first."

"Of course I do or I never would have asked you to watch my children. They're far more precious to me than any plane." His eyes went hard, leaving no room for doubt. Any mistakes with his son and daughter would not be tolerated. Then he looked back at the sky, mellow Seth returning. "Why not manage a gallery if you need to fill your hours?"

Because she would be lucky if working in a gallery would cover rent on an apartment or a lease on an economy car, much less food and economic stability. Because she wanted to prove she didn't need a man to be successful. And most importantly, *because* she didn't ever again want the freaked out feeling of being less than six hundred dollars away from bankruptcy.

Okay, sort of melodramatic since she'd still owned jewelry she could hock. But still scary as hell when she'd sold off her house and car only to find it barely covered the existing loans.

"I do not expect anyone to support me, and given the current economy, jobs in the arts aren't exactly filling up the want ad sections. Bethany has experience in the business, while I bring new contacts to the table. We're a good team. Besides, I really do enjoy this work, strange as that may seem. While A-1 has employees who handle cleaning most of the time, I pitch in if someone's out sick or we get the call for a special job. I enjoy the break from office work."

"Okay, I believe you. So you used to like art history, and now you enjoy feeding people's Evian habits and their need for clean armrests."

The deepening sarcasm in his voice had her spine starching with irritation. "Are you making fun of me for the hell of it or is there a purpose behind this line of questioning?"

"I always have a purpose," he said as smoothly as he flew the plane. "Will your whim of the week pass, once you realize people take these services for granted and your work is not appreciated? What happens to my aircraft then? I'll be stuck wading through that stack of proposals all over again."

He really saw her as a flighty, spoiled individual and that stung. It wasn't particularly fair, either. "Do you keep flying even when people don't appreciate a smooth or on-time flight, when they only gripe about the late or bumpy rides?"

"I'm not following your point here. I like to fly. Are you saying you like to clean?"

"I like to restore order," she answered simply, truthfully.

The shrinks she'd seen as a teen had helped her rechannel the need for perfection her mother had drilled into Alexa from birth. She'd stopped starving herself, eased off searching the art world for flawless beauty and now took comfort from order, from peace.

"Ah—" a smile spread over his face "—you like control. Now that I understand."

"Who doesn't like control?" And how many therapy sessions had she spent on *that* topic?

He looked over at her with an emerald-eyed sexy stare. The air crackled as if a lightning bolt had zipped between them. "Would you like to take over flying the plane?"

"Are you kidding?" She slid her hands under her thighs even though she couldn't deny to herself just how tempting the offer sounded.

Who wouldn't want to take a stab at soaring through the air, just her and the wide-open blue rolling out in front of the plane? It would be like driving a car alone for the first time. Pushing an exotic Arabian racehorse to gallop. Happier memories from another lifetime called to her.

"Just take the yoke."

God, how she wanted to, but there was something in his voice that gave her pause. She couldn't quite figure out his game. She wasn't in the position to risk her livelihood or her newfound independence on some guy's whims.

"Your children are on board." She knew she sounded prim, but then hey, she was a nanny for the day.

"If it appears you're about to send us into a nosedive, I'll take over."

"Maybe another time." She leaped up from the seat, not about to get sucked into a false sense of control that wouldn't last. "I think I hear Olivia."

His low chuckle followed her all the way back to both peacefully sleeping children.

Alexa could hear his husky laugh echoing in her ears two hours later as they settled into their luxurious hotel room in St. Augustine, Florida.

She had seen the best of the best lodgings and the Casa Monica—one of the oldest hotels in the United States—was gorgeous by any standards, designed to resemble a castle. The city of St. Augustine itself was rich with history and ornate Spanish architecture, the Casa Monica being a jewel. The hotel had been built in the 1800s, named for St. Monica, the mother of St. Augustine, the city's namesake.

And here she was with Seth and his babies. She could use a little motherly advice from a patron saint's mom right now.

She also needed to find some time to touch base with Bethany at work. Even though she was sure Bethany could manage—it had been her company at one time—she really did need to speak with her partner and give Bethany her contact information.

Seth had checked them into one of the penthouse suites, with a walk-out to a turret with views of the city. The suite had two bedrooms connected by a sitting area. The mammoth bath with a circular tub called to her muscles, which ached from working all day then lugging one of the baby carriers around. Then her thoughts went to images of sharing the tub with a man…not just any man…

She turned back to the room, decorated in blue velvet upholstery and heavy brocade curtains. Seth had claimed the spare bedroom, leaving her the larger master with two cribs inside. She trailed her fingers over the handle to Olivia's car seat on the floor beside the mission style sofa in the sitting room. Olivia's brother rested in his car seat next to hers.

"Your twins sleep well. They're making this job too easy, you know."

"Pippa doesn't believe in bedtimes. They usually nap hard their first day with me." Seth strode into the spare bedroom. "Expect mayhem soon enough when they wake up recharged. Owen's a charmer, so much so it's easy to miss the mischief he's plotting. He's always looking for the best way to stack furniture and climb his way out. You can see where he's already had stitches through his left eyebrow. As for Olivia, well, keep a close eye on her hands. She loves to collect small things to shove up her nose, in her ears, in her mouth…"

Affection swelled from each word as he detailed his children's personalities. The man definitely loosened up when around his kids or when he was talking about them. He seemed to know his offspring well. Not what she would have expected from a distant dad. Intrigued, she moved closer.

Through the open door, she could see him drape his suit coat on the foot of the bed. He loosened his tie further and unbuttoned his collar, then worked the buttons free down his shirt.

Alexa backed toward her own room. "Um, what are you doing?"

Seth slipped his still-knotted tie over his head and untucked the shirt. "Owen kicked his shoes against me when I picked him up after we landed." He pointed to smudges down the left side. "I need to change fast before my meeting."

His all-important meeting. Right. Seth had told her he was having dinner with a bigwig contact downstairs and she could order whatever she wanted from room service. He would be back in two to three hours. If she could get the kids settled in the tub, she could sit on the side and make some work calls while watching them. Check voice mail and email on her iPhone, deal with the standard million missed calls from her mom before moving on to deal with work. Her staff wasn't large, just four other employees, including Bethany. Her partner was slowing down, but could hold down the fort. In the event an emergency arose, Bethany would make sure things didn't reach a boiling point. So she was in the free and clear to spend the night here. With the kids.

And Seth.

She thumbed a smudge from the base of the brass lamp. "Can't have shoe prints all over you at the big meeting. That's for sure."

"Could you look in the hang-up bag and get me another shirt?"

"Right, okay." She spun away before he undressed further. She charged over to the black suitcase resting on top of a mahogany luggage rack.

Alexa tugged the zipper around and...oh my. The scent of him wafted up from his clothes, which should be impossible since they were clean clothes. But no question about it, the suitcase had captured the essence of him and it was intoxicating.

Her fingers moved along the hangers until she found a plain white shirt mixed in with a surprising amount of colorful others. Mr. Buttoned-up Businessman had a wild side. An unwelcome tingle played along her skin and in her imagination. She slapped the case closed.

Shirt in hand, she turned back to Seth who was now wearing only his pants and a T-shirt. His shoulders stretched the fabric to the limit. Her fingers curled into the shirt in her hands, her fingertips registering Sea Island Cotton, high-end, breathable, known for keeping the wearer's body cool throughout the day.

Maybe she could use some Sea Island Cotton herself because she was heating up.

Alexa thrust the shirt toward him. "Will this do?"

"Great, thanks." His knuckles brushed hers as she passed over his clothes as if they were intimately sharing a space.

And more.

Awareness chased up her wrist, her arm, higher still as the intimacy of the moment engulfed her. She was in a gorgeous hotel room, with a hot man and his beautiful children, helping him get dressed. The scene was too wonderful. Too close to what she'd once dreamed of having with her ex.

She jerked back fast. "Any last minute things to tell me about the kids when I order up supper?"

"Owen is allergic to strawberries, but Olivia loves them and if she can get her hands on them, she tries to share them with her brother. So watch that—hotels do the strawberry garnish thing on meals."

"Anything else?" She tried to pull her eyes away

from the nimble glide of his fingers up the buttons on his shirt.

"If you have an emergency, you can contact me at this number." He grabbed a hotel pen and jotted a string of numbers on the back of a business card. "That's my private cell line I use only for the kids."

"Got it." She tucked it in the corner of the gold gilded mirror. She could handle a couple of babies for a few hours.

Right?

"Don't lose it. And don't let Owen find it or he will eat it." He unbuckled his belt.

Her jaw dropped.

He tucked in his shirttails—and caught her staring. Her face heating, she turned away. Again.

Looking out the window seemed like a safe idea even though she'd been to St. Augustine about a dozen times. She could see Flagler College across the way, a place she'd once considered attending. Except her parents refused to pay if she left Charleston. Students at the Flagler castlelike fortress must feel as if they were attending Hogwarts. In fact, the whole city had a removed-from-reality feel, a step out of time. Much like this entire trip.

A Cinderella carriage pulled by a horse creaked slowly by as a Mercedes convertible whipped around and past it.

As Charleston had the French Huguenot influence, buildings here sported a Spanish Renaissance flair, and if Seth didn't get dressed soon, she would run out of things to look at. He was too much of a threat to her world for her to risk a tempting peek.

Her body hummed with awareness even when she

didn't see him. What a hell of a time for her hormones to stoke to life again.

"You can turn around now." Seth's voice stroked along her ragged nerves.

She chewed her lip, spinning back to face him, a man too handsome for his own good—or hers. "I've taken care of babies before."

Not often, but for friends in hopes she could prepare herself for the day it was her turn. A day that had never come around.

"Twins are different." He tugged the tie back over his head.

If he was so worried, he should cancel his meeting. She wanted to snap at him, but knew her irritability for what it was. Her perfect plan for the day had gone way off course, complicated even more by how damn attracted she was to the man she wanted to woo for a contract, not as a bed partner.

Memories of rustling sheets and sweat-slicked bodies smoked through her mind. She'd had a healthy sex life with her ex, so much so that she hadn't considered something could be wrong until everything fell apart. She definitely couldn't trust her body to judge the situation.

"Seth," she said his first name so easily she almost gasped, but forced herself to continue, "the twins and I will manage. We'll eat applesauce and fries and chicken nuggets then skyrocket your pay-per-view bill with cartoon movies until our brains are mush. I'll watch Olivia with small objects, and Owen's charm won't distract me from his climbing or strawberry snitching. They'll be fine. Go to your meeting."

He actually hesitated before grabbing his jacket from

the edge of the bed. "I'll be downstairs in the bar if you need me."

Oh, her body needed him all right. Too much for her own good. She was better off using her brains.

Seth stepped from the elevator into the lobby full of arches that led to the bar and restaurant. He scanned the chairs and sofas of rich dark woods with red-striped fabrics. Looking further, he searched past the heavy beams and thick curtains pulled back at each archway.

Thank God, somehow he'd managed to make it here ahead of his dinner partner. He strode past an iron fountain with Moorish tiles toward the bar where he was supposed to meet Javier Cortez, a cousin to royalty.

Literally. Cortez was related to the Medina family, a European monarchy that had ended in a violent coup. The Medinas and relatives had relocated to the United States, living in anonymity until a media scoop exposed their royal roots last year.

Cortez had served as head of security to one of the princes prior to the newsbreak and now oversaw safety measures for the entire family. Landing the Medinas as clients would be a huge coup.

Seth hitched up onto a stool at the bar, waving to the bartender for a seltzer water. Nothing stronger tonight.

Jansen Jets was still a small company, relatively speaking, but thanks to an in, he'd landed this meeting. One of those "Human Web" six degrees of separation moments—his cousin's wife's sister married into the Landis family, and a Landis brother married the illegitimate Medina princess.

Okay, that was more like ten degrees of separation. Thankfully, enough to bring him to this meeting. From this point on he had to rest on his own merits. Much like he'd told Alexa. *Alexa*...

Damn it all, did every thought have to circle back around to her?

Sure he'd noticed her on a physical level when he'd first stepped on the plane, and he'd managed the attraction well enough until he'd caught her eyes sliding over his body as he'd undone his pants. The ensuing heat wave sure hadn't been a welcome condition right before a meeting.

But he needed her help, so he would damn well wrestle the attraction into submission. His kids were his number one priority. He'd tried calling his ex multiple times since landing in St. Augustine, but only got her voice mail. Life had been a hell of a lot less complicated when he was flying those routes solo in North Dakota.

There didn't seem to be a damn thing more he could do about his mess of a personal life. Hopefully he could at least make headway in the business world.

Starting now.

The elevator dinged, doors swished open and Javier Cortez stepped out. Predictably the bar patrons buzzed. The newness of having royalty around hadn't worn off for people. The forty-year-old royal cousin strode out confidently, his Castilian heritage fitting right into the hotel's decor.

The guy's regal lineage didn't matter to Seth. He just appreciated the guy's hard-nosed efficiency. This deal would be sewn up quickly, one way or another.

"Sorry I'm late." Cortez thrust out his hand. "Javier Cortez."

"Seth Jansen." He stood to shake Javier's hand and then resettled onto a barstool beside the other guy.

The bartender placed an amber drink in front of Javier before he even placed an order. "I appreciate your flying down to meet with me here." He rattled the ice and looked around with assessing eyes. "My wife loves this place."

"I can see why. Lots of historic appeal."

It was also a good locale to conduct business, near the Medinas' private island off the coast of Florida. Although Seth hadn't been invited into that inner sanctum yet. Security measures were tight. No one knew the exact location and few had seen the island fortress. The Medinas owned a couple of private jets, but were looking to increase their transport options to and from the island as their family expanded with marriages and new children.

Cortez tasted his drink and set it on the cocktail napkin. "Since my wife and I are still technically finishing up our honeymoon, I promised her a longer stay, the chance to shop, laze around by the pool, soak up some Florida sun before we head back to Boston."

What the hell was he supposed to say to that? "Congratulations."

"Thanks, thanks. I hear you have your kids and their sitter with you."

Of course he'd heard, even though Seth had only been in town for about an hour. The guy was a security whiz and obviously didn't walk into a meeting unprepared. "I like to work in time with them whenever I can, so I brought the kids and Mary Poppins along."

"Excellent. Then you won't mind if we postpone the rest of this discussion."

Crap. Just what he didn't need.

The stay here extended. Less taken care of tonight, more tomorrow and even the next day. "Of course."

Cortez stood, taking his drink with him as he started back toward the elevator. Seth abandoned his seltzer water.

They stepped into the elevator together, and Cortez swiped his card for the penthouse level. "My wife and I would enjoy having you and your kids meet us for breakfast in the morning, your sitter, too. Around nine? Great," he said without waiting for an answer. "See you there."

Holy hell. Breakfast in a restaurant with a one-year-old was tough enough. But with two of them?

He stepped out onto the top floor, Javier going right as he went left.

The closer he came to the suite's door, the louder the muffled sounds grew. Squealing babies. Damn. Was one of them hurt? He double-timed toward his room, whipped the key card through just as the door opened.

Alexa carried a baby on each hip—two freshly bathed and wet naked babies. Her cheeks were flushed, her smile wide. "I just caught them. Holy cow, they've got some speed for toddlers."

He snagged a towel from the arm of the sofa and held it open. "Pass me one."

She handed Owen over and Seth saw…

Her shirt was soaking wet, clinging to every perfect curve. Who would have thought Mary Poppins could rock the hell out of a wet T-shirt contest?

Three

Alexa plucked at her wet company shirt, conscious of the way it clung to her breasts. She didn't need the heat in Seth's eyes. She didn't need the answering fire it stirred in her. They both had different goals for what remained of their twenty-four-hour deal. They were best served focusing on the children and work.

Turning away, she hitched Olivia up on her hip and snagged the other towel from where she'd dropped it on the sofa to chase the racing duo around the suite. "You're back early from your dinner meeting."

"You need some clothes." The sound of his confident footsteps sounded softly behind her on plush carpet.

"Dry ones, for sure." She glanced through to the bathroom. Towels were draped on the floor around the circular tub, soaking up all the splashes. "I let the babies use the Jacuzzi like a kiddie pool. A few plastic cups and they were happy to play. Supper should be arriving soon. I thought you were room service when I heard you at the door."

"They'll need cleaning up again after supper." He tugged out two diapers and two T-shirts from the diaper bag.

"Then I'll just order more towels." She plucked the tiny pink T-shirt from his hand and busied herself with dressing Olivia to keep from noticing how at ease he was handling his squirming son.

"Fair enough." He pressed the diaper tapes in place, his large masculine hands surprisingly nimble.

"Did your meeting go well?" She wrestled a tiny waving arm through the sleeve.

"We didn't get through more than half a drink. He had to postpone until the morning." A quick tug later, he had Owen's powder-blue shirt in place. He hoisted his son in the air and buzzed his belly before setting him on his feet. "I'll just call room service and add my order to the rest."

He wasn't going back to work? They would be spending the rest of the evening here. Together with the children, of course. And after the toddlers drifted off? He'd mentioned Pippa kept them up late. With luck the pint-size chaperones would burn the midnight oil.

"Too bad your dinner companion couldn't have told you about the delay before you left Charleston. You would have had time to make other arrangements for the children." And she would have been at home in her lonely apartment eating ice cream while thinking about encountering Seth on his plane. Because without question, he was a memorable man.

"I'm glad to have the time with them. I assume you can arrange to stay longer?"

"I'll call my partner back as soon as the kids are asleep. She and I will make it work."

"Excellent. Now we just need to arrange extra clothes and toiletries for you." He reached for the room phone as Olivia and Owen chased each other in circles around their father. "When I order my supper I'll also have the concierge pick up something for you to change int—"

"Really, no need." She held up a hand, an unsettling tingle tripping up her spine at the thought of wearing things purchased by him. "I'll wear the hotel robe tonight and we can have the hotel wash my clothes. The kids and I will kill time tomorrow browsing around downtown, shopping while you finish your meeting. You do have a double stroller, don't you?"

"Already arranged. But you are going to need a change of clothing sooner than that." The furrows in his brow warned her a second before he said, "My business prospect wants to have breakfast with the kids and there's not a chance in hell I can carry that off on my own. It's my fault you're here without a change of clothes."

A business breakfast? With two toddlers? Whose genius idea was that? But she held her silence and conceded to the need for something appropriate to wear.

She stifled a twinge of nerves at discussing her clothing size. She was past those days of stepping on the scales every morning for her mom to check—what a hell of a way to spend "mother-daughter" time. And thank God, she was past the days of starving herself into a size zero.

Size zero. There'd been an irony in that, as if she could somehow fade away...

Blinking the past back, she said, "Okay then, tell them to buy smalls or eights, and my shoes are size seven."

His green eyes glimmered wickedly. "And underwear measurements?"

She poked him in the chest with one finger. "Not on your life am I answering that one." God, his chest was solid. She stepped away. "Make sure to keep a tally of how much everything costs. I insist on reimbursing you."

"Unnecessarily prideful, but as you wish," he said it so arrogantly she wanted to thump him on the back of his head.

Not a wise business move, though, touching him again. One little tap had nearly seared her fingertip and her mind. "I pay my own way now."

"At least let me loan you a T-shirt to sleep in tonight rather than that stifling hotel robe."

His clothes against her naked flesh?

Whoa.

Shaking off the goose bumps, she followed the toddling twins into the master bedroom. The rumble of his voice followed her as Seth ordered his meal, her clothing and some other toiletries...

Olivia and Owen sprinted to check out the matching portable cribs that had been set up on the far side of the king-size bed, each neatly made. Everything had been provided to accommodate a family. A real family. Except she would crawl under her own covers all alone wearing a hot guy's T-shirt.

Alexa wrapped her arms around her stomach, reminded

of the life she'd been denied with the implosion of her marriage. A life she purposefully hadn't thought about in a year since she'd craved a real family more than her next breath. Being thrust into this situation with Seth stirred longings she'd ignored for too long. Damn it, she'd taken this gamble for her company, her employees, her future.

But in doing so, she hadn't realized how deeply playing at this family game could cut into her heart.

Playing pretend family was kicking his ass.

Seth forked up the last bite of his Chilean sea bass while Alexa started her warm peach bread pudding with lavender cream. They'd opted to feed the babies first and put them to bed so the adults could actually dine in peace out on the turret balcony. Their supper had been set up by the wrought-iron table for two, complete with a lone rose in the middle of the table. Historical sconces on either side of the open doors cast a candlelit glow over the table.

Classical music drifted softly from inside. Okay, so it was actually something called "The Mozart Effect—Music for Babies," and he used it to help soothe Olivia and Owen to sleep. But it still qualified as mood-setting music for grown-ups.

And holy crap, did Alexa ever qualify as a smoking hot adult.

She'd changed into one of his T-shirts with the fluffy hotel robe over it. She looked as if she'd just rolled out of his bed. An ocean breeze lifted her whispery blond hair as late evening street noises echoed softly from the street below. Tonight had been the closest he'd come to experiencing family life with his children.

He hadn't dated much since his divorce and when he had, he'd been careful to keep that world separate from his kids. Working side by side with Alexa had more than cut the tasks in half tonight. That made him angry all over again that he'd screwed up so badly in his own marriage. He and Pippa had known it was a long shot going in, but they'd both wanted to give it a chance, for the babies. Or at least that's what he'd thought, until he'd discovered Pippa wasn't even sure if he was the biological father.

His gut twisted.

Damn it all, Olivia and Owen were *his* children. *His* name was on their birth certificate. And he refused to let anyone take them from him. Pippa vowed she wasn't going to challenge the custody agreement, but she'd lied to him before, and in such a major way, he had trouble trusting her.

He studied the woman across from him, wishing he could read her thoughts better, but she held herself in such tight control at all times. Sure, he knew he couldn't judge all females by how things had shaken down between him and Pippa. But it definitely made him wary. Fool him once, shame on her. Fool him twice. Shame on him.

Alexa Randall was here for one reason only. To use him to jump-start her business. She wasn't in St. Augustine to play house. She didn't know, much less love, his kids. She was doing a job. Everybody in this world had an agenda. As long as he kept that knowledge forefront in his mind, they would be fine.

He reached for his seltzer water. "You're good with kids."

"Thanks," she said tightly, stabbing at her pudding.

"Seriously. You'll make a good mother someday."

She shook her head and shoved away her half-eaten dessert. "I prefer to have a husband for that and my only attempt at marriage didn't end well."

The bitterness in her voice hung between them.

He tipped back his crystal glass, eyeing her over the rim. "I'm really sorry to hear that."

Sighing, she dipped her finger in the water and traced the rim of her glass until the crystal sang. "I married a guy who seemed perfect. He didn't even care about my family's money. In fact, he sided with my dad about signing a prenup to prove it." Faster and faster her finger moved, the pitch growing higher. "After always having to second-guess friendships while growing up, that felt so good—thinking he loved me for myself, unconditionally."

"That's how it's supposed to work."

"Supposed to. But then, I'm sure you understand what it's like to have to question everyone's motives."

"Not always. I grew up in a regular farming family in North Dakota. Everyone around me had working class values. I spent my spare time camping, fishing or flying."

"Most of my friends in private school wanted the perks of hanging out with me—shopping trips in New York. For my sixteenth, my mother flew me and my friends to the Bahamas." She tapped the glass once with a short fingernail. "The ones with parents who could afford the same kind of perks were every bit as spoiled as I was. No wonder I didn't have any true friends."

Having to question people's motives as an adult was tough enough. But worrying as a kid? That could mark a person long-term. He thought of his children asleep in the next room and wondered how he would keep their lives even-keeled.

"So your ex seems like a dream guy with the prenup… and…?"

"His only condition was that I not take any money from my family." Her eyes took on a faraway, jaded look that bothered him more than it should have for someone he'd just met. "My money could go into trust for our kids someday, but we would live our lives on what we made. Sounded good, honorable."

"What happened?" He lifted his glass.

"I was allergic to his sperm."

He choked on his water. "Uh, could you run that by me again?"

"You heard me. Allergic to his swimmers. We can both have kids, just not with each other." She folded her arms on the edge of the table, leaning closer. "I was sad when the doctor told me, but I figured, hey, this was our call to adopt. Apparently Travis—my ex—didn't get the same message."

"Let me get this straight." Seth placed his glass on the table carefully to keep from snapping the stemware in two with his growing anger. "Your ex-husband left you because the two of you couldn't have biological children together?"

"Bingo," she said with a tight smile that didn't come close to reaching her haunted blue eyes.

"He sounds like a shallow jerk." A jerk Seth had an urge to punch for putting such deep shadows in this woman's eyes. "I would be happy to kick his ass for you. I may be a desk jockey these days, but I've still got enough North Dakota farm boy in me to take him down."

A smile played at her lips. "No worries. I kick butts on my own these days."

"Good for you." He admired her resilience, her spunk. She'd rebuilt her life after two nearly simultaneous blows from life that would have debilitated most people.

"I try not to beat myself up about it." Sagging back in the wrought-iron patio chair, she clutched the robe closed with her fists. "I didn't have much practice in making smart choices about the people I invited into my life. So it stands to reason I would screw that one up, too."

"Well, I'm a damn good judge of character and it's obvious to me that *he* screwed up." Seth reached across the table and touched her elbow lightly where the sleeve fell back to reveal the vulnerable crook. "Not you."

Her eyes opened wider with surprise, with awareness, but she didn't pull away. "Thanks for the vote of confidence, but I know there had to be fault on both sides."

"Still, that's not always easy to see or say." His hand fell away.

"What about *your* ex?" She straightened the extra fork she hadn't needed for her dinner. In fact, she hadn't eaten much of her fire-grilled sea scallops at all and only half of her bread pudding. Maybe the cuisine here didn't suit her. "Does she make it a regular practice to run off and leave the kids?"

"Actually, no." Pippa was usually diligent when it came to their care. In fact, she usually cried buckets anytime she left them.

Alexa tapped the top of his hand with a whisper-soft touch. "Come on now. I unloaded about my sucky marriage story. What's yours?"

Normally he preferred not to talk about his failures. But the moonlight, good food—for him at least—and even better company made him want to extend the evening. If that meant spilling a few public knowledge facts about his personal life, then so be it.

"There's no great drama to share—" And yeah, he was lying, but he preferred to keep it low-key. He was used to glossing over the truth in front of his kids, who were too young to understand paternity questions. "We had a fling that resulted in a surprise pregnancy—" Pippa had just failed to mention the other fling she'd had around the same time. "So we got married for the children, gave it an honest try and figured out it wasn't going to work. We already had divorce papers in motion by the time the babies were due."

"If you don't mind my asking—" she paused until he waved her on "—why did you get married at all then?"

He'd asked himself the same question more than once, late at night when he was alone and missing the twins. "Old-fashioned, I guess. I wanted to be around my kids all the time. I wanted it to work." Wanted the babies to be his. "It just…didn't."

"You're so calm about it," she said with more of those shadows chasing around in her eyes.

Calm? He was a holy mess inside, but letting that anger, the betrayal, fly wouldn't accomplish anything. "I have the twins. Pippa and I are trying to be good parents. At least I thought we were."

Her hand covered his completely, steadily. "By all appearances you're doing a great job. They're beautiful, sweet babies."

The touch of her soft skin sent a bolt of lust straight through his veins, pumping pulsing blood south. He wrestled his thoughts back to the conversation, back to the care of his offspring. "They're hell on wheels, but I would do anything for them. Anything."

So there was no need for him to stress over the fact that Alexa turned him on so hard his teeth hurt. He'd been too long without sex, only a couple of encounters in the year since his divorce. That had to be the reason for his instantaneous, out of control reaction to this woman.

Gauging by the pure blue flame in her eyes, she was feeling it, too.

He was realizing they had a lot more than just a hefty dose of attraction in common. They were both reeling from crappy marriages and completely focused on their careers. Neither of them was looking for anything permanent that would involve more messy emotions.

So why not hook up? If he wanted to act on their attraction and she was cool with the fact that being together had no effect on his business decisions, this could be the best damn thing to happen to him in months. *She* could be the best thing to happen to him in months.

Yeah, this could work.

Simple, uncomplicated sex.

They had an empty second bedroom waiting for them. He always carried condoms these days. One surprise pregnancy was enough. They had moonlight, atmosphere. She was even already half-undressed. There was nothing stopping him from seeing if she was amenable.

Decision made, Seth pulled the rose from the vase and stroked it lightly down her nose. Her eyes blinked wide with surprise, but she didn't say a word, didn't so much as move. Hell, yeah.

Emboldened, he traced her lips with the bud before he leaned across the table and kissed her.

Four

The warm press of Seth's mouth against hers surprised Alexa into stillness—for all of three heartbeats. Then her pulse double-timed. Surprise became desire. The attraction she'd been feeling since first laying eyes on him, since he'd taken off his tie, since she'd felt the steamy glide of his gaze over her damp clothing now ramped into hyperdrive.

He stood without breaking contact, and she rose with him as they stepped around the small table into each other's arms. She gripped his shoulders, her fingers sinking into the warm cotton of the shirt she'd chosen for him earlier. Her defenses were low, without a doubt. The romantic meal, moonlit turret and alluring dinner companion had lulled her. Even the soft classical music stroked over her tensed and frazzled nerves. It had been so long since she'd relaxed, too busy charging ahead with rebuilding her life. Even opening up about her divorce had felt—if not good—at least cathartic.

It had also left her bare and defenseless.

The man might be brusque in the way he spoke sometimes, but, wow, did he ever take his time with a kiss. She slid one hand from his shoulder up to the back of his neck, her fingers toying with the coarse texture of his hair. Her body fit against his, her softness giving way to the hard planes of his chest. The sensitive pads of her fingers savored the rasp of his late day beard as she traced his strong jaw, brushed across his cheekbones and back into his thick hair.

His mouth moved over hers firmly, surely, enticing her to open for him. Her breasts pressed more firmly against him as she breathed faster and faster with arousal. The scent of aftershave mingled with the salty sea air. The taste of lime water and spices from his dinner flavored their kiss, tempting her senses all the more to throw reason away. The bold sweep of his tongue made her hunger for more of this. More of *him*.

How easy it would be to follow him into his bedroom and toss away all the stress and worries of the past years as quickly as discarded clothes. Except, too soon, morning would come and with it would come all those concerns, multiplied because of their lack of self-control.

God, this was so reckless and unwise and impulsive in a way she couldn't afford any longer. Scavenging for a shred of self-control, she pushed at his shoulders since she couldn't seem to bring herself to tear her mouth away from his.

Thank goodness he took the hint.

He pulled back, but not far, only a whisper away.

Each breath she took drew in the crisp scent of him. The starlight reflected in his green eyes staring at her with a keen perception of how very much she ached to take this kiss further.

Her chest pumped for air even though she knew full well the dizziness had nothing to do with oxygen and everything to do with Seth's appeal. Slowly he guided her back to her chair—good thing since her legs were wobbly—and he returned to his as well, his eyes still holding her captive. He lifted his crystal glass, sipping the sparkling water while watching her over the rim.

She forced a laugh that came out half strangled. "That was unexpected."

"Really?" He placed his glass on the table again. The pulse visibly throbbing in his neck offered the only sign he was as shaken as she was by what they'd just shared. "I've wanted to kiss you since I first saw you on board my plane. At that moment, I thought that attraction was mutual. Now, I *know* it is."

His cool arrogance smoked across the table.

A chilling thought iced the heat just as quickly as he'd stoked it. "Is that why you asked me to watch your children? Because you wanted a chance to hit on me?" She sat straighter in her chair and wished she wore something more businesslike than a borrowed terry-cloth robe and his shirt. "I thought we had a business arrangement. Mixing business and personal lives is never a good idea."

"Then why did you kiss me back?" He turned the glass on the tablecloth.

"Impulse."

His eyes narrowed. "So you admit you're attracted to me."

Duh. Denying the mutual draw would be pointless. "You know that I am, but it doesn't mean I've been making plans to act on the feeling. I think Brad Pitt's hot as hell, but I wouldn't jump him even if given the opportunity."

"You think I'm Brad Pitt-hot?"

Damn the return of his arrogant grin.

"I was just making a point," she snapped.

"But you think I'm hot."

"Not relevant." She flattened her hands on the table. "I'm not acting on the impulse any further tonight or ever. If that means you renege on your offer to read my proposal and refer me to others in the business, then so be it. I will not sleep my way into a deal."

She pushed to her feet.

"Whoa, hold on." Standing, he circled the table to face her, stroking her upper arm soothingly. "I didn't mean to imply anything of the sort. First, I don't believe you're the kind of person to get ahead in the world that way. And second, I have never paid for sex, and I never intend to."

She froze, his touch sending fresh skitters of awareness up her arm. The darkness and distant night sounds isolated them with too much intimacy.

Alexa eased back a step toward their suite and the soft serenade of Mozart on the breeze. "Have you looked into finding someone else to take care of your children?"

Still, he didn't move. He didn't have to. His presence called to her as he simply stood a couple of steps away, his broad shoulders backlit by the moon, starlight playing across his blond hair, giving him a Greek godlike air.

"Why would I need to do that?" he asked. "You're here for them."

"Our agreement only lasts for twenty-four hours," she reminded him, holding onto the door frame to bolster her wavering resolve.

"I thought we established the time frame had expanded because my meeting with Javier Cortez fell through tonight." He stepped closer, stopping just shy of touching her again. "You even rearranged things at your work to accommodate our business agreement."

He was right, and she'd allowed him to scramble her thoughts once more. She locked onto his last three words and pushed ahead. "Our *business* agreement."

"You're angry."

"Not…angry exactly. Just frustrated and disappointed in both of us."

His eyes flared with something indefinable. "Disappointed?"

"Oh—" she suddenly understood his expression "—not disappointed in the kiss. It was… Hell, you were here, too. There's no denying the chemistry between us."

Another arrogant grin spread across his face. "I agree one hundred percent."

"But back to the Brad Pitt principle." She stiffened her spine and her resolve. "Just because there's an attraction doesn't mean it's wise to act on it. I'm disappointed that we did something so reckless, so unprofessional. My business has to be my primary focus, just as you've said your children are your main concern."

"Having my priorities in order doesn't cancel out my attraction to you. I can separate business from pleasure." He held her with his laser hot gaze. "I'm very good at multitasking."

Anger did build inside her now alongside the frustration. "You're not hearing me! This thing between us is too much, too soon. We barely know each other and we both have high stakes riding on this trip." She jabbed him in the chest with one finger. "So, listen closely. No. More. Kissing."

She launched through the door and into the suite before he could shake her resolve again. But as she raced across the luxurious sitting area into her bedroom, his voice echoed in her ears and through her hungry senses.

"Damn shame."

She completely agreed. Sleep tonight would be difficult to come by as regrets piled on top of frustrated desire.

Staring off over the city skyline, Seth leaned back in his chair, staying on the turret balcony long after Alexa left. The heat of their kiss still sizzling through him, he finished his seltzer water, waiting for the light in her room to turn off.

He'd only met her today, and he couldn't recall wanting any woman this much. The strength of the attraction had been strong enough on its own. But now that he'd actually tasted her? He pushed the glass aside, his deeper thirst not even close to quenched.

Now he had to decide what to do about that feeling. She was right in saying that giving in to an affair wasn't wise. They both had important reasons to keep their acquaintance all business.

His life was complicated enough. He needed to keep

his life stable for his kids. No parade of women through the door, confusing them.

He eyed his smartphone on the table where it had been resting since his four attempts to contact Pippa. She still wasn't returning his messages, and his temper was starting to simmer. What if there had been something wrong with one of the kids and he needed to contact her? She should at least pick up to find out why he was trying to reach her.

His phone vibrated with an incoming call. He slammed his chair back on all four legs and scooped up his cell fast. The LED screen showed a stored name... his cousin Paige back in Charleston.

Not Pippa.

Damn it.

Even his extended family kept in better contact with him than the mother of his kids. His cousins Paige and Vic had both moved from North Dakota, each starting their families in the Charleston area. With no other family left out west, Seth had followed and started his own business.

He picked up without hesitation. "Paige? Everything okay?"

"We're fine." His cousin's voice was soft as if lowered to keep from waking her children. Classical guitar music played softly in the background. "The girls are both finally asleep. I've been worried about you all afternoon. How are you and the twins? I feel so bad that I couldn't help you out."

"No need to call and apologize. We prefer to steer clear of strep throat."

"Actually I'm calling about Vic and Claire..."

Oh. Hell. In the chaos with the twins, he'd actually

forgotten that his cousin Vic's wife had gone into labor today. "How's she doing?"

"She delivered a healthy baby boy just before midnight. Nine pounds thirteen ounces, which explains the C-section. But Mom and baby are doing great. His big sister and big brother can't wait to meet him in the morning." Two boys and a girl. A family.

Seth scratched the kink in his neck. "Send my congratulations when you see them. I'll swing by for a visit when I get back in town."

"I'll let them know." The reception crackled as it sounded like she moved her phone to the other ear. More guitar music filled the airwaves... Bach, perhaps? "Actually, I called for a different reason. Now that Claire's had the baby and Vic has picked up their kids, her sister Starr says she can watch the twins. They know her two kids. They'll have a blast. You could fly Olivia and Owen up early in the morning before your first meeting."

"That's a generous offer..."

"My girls won't be contagious in another day or two once the antibiotics kick in, so I can relieve her then. No worries."

Her plan sounded workable. And yet, he hesitated, his gaze drawn back to the suite where Alexa slept. "You're all busy with your own families, and I have a plan in place here."

"You're family," Paige insisted sincerely. "We want to help."

"I appreciate that." Except he genuinely wanted his kids near him—and he wanted to keep Alexa near him, too.

The thought of cutting his time with Alexa short—it just wasn't happening. Crazy, really, since he could contact her later, after this deal was cinched. If she was even still speaking to him once she realized he never intended to give her the Jansen Jets contract.

No. His time to get to know Alexa was now. He needed to figure out this unrelenting draw between them and work through it. She was here, and he intended to keep it that way. "Thanks, Paige, but I meant it when I said I'm set. I have help."

"Hmm…" Her voice rose with interest. "You have a new nanny?"

His family chipped in most of the time, but he didn't want to take advantage so he hired a couple of part-time nannies on occasion, all of which Paige would already know about. "Not a nanny. More of a sitter, a, uh, friend actually."

"A female friend?" she pressed, tenacious as ever.

"She's a female, yes." *Definitely* female.

"That's it?" Paige laughed. "That's all you're going to tell me, eh?"

"There's not much to tell." Yet. His eyes drifted back to the suite as he envisioned Alexa curled up asleep, wearing his shirt.

"Ah," she said smugly, "so you're still in the early stages, but not too early, right, or she wouldn't be there with your children. Because, as best as I can remember, you haven't dated much and none of those women ever got anywhere near the twins."

His cousin was too insightful. The way she homed in on the intensity of his draw to Alexa so quickly made him uncomfortable.

He shot up from his seat. "That's enough hypothesizing about my personal life for one night. I need to go."

"I'm not giving up. I'll want details when you return,"

Paige insisted, getting louder and louder by the second. "And I want to meet her. I know you guard your privacy, but I'm family and I love you."

"Love you too, cuz."

"So you'll talk to me? Let me know what's going on in your world rather than hole up the way you did after Pippa—"

"I hear a kid," he cut her short. "Gotta go. Bye." He thumbed the off button and flipped the phone in his palm, over and over.

Guilt kicked around in his gut for shutting down Paige and for taking advantage of Alexa's help. He should send Alexa back to Charleston and then impose on the sister of a cousin-in-law because his ex-wife had dumped his kids off without warning...

Hell, his life was screwed up, and he needed to start taking charge. He'd meant it when he said he could separate the personal from the professional. But he also heard Alexa when she said this was moving too fast for her. She needed more time, time they wouldn't have if she went back to Charleston while he stayed here. He suspected once she went home, she would erect mile-high walls between them, especially once she learned he'd never planned to sign her cleaning company.

He needed longer with her *now*.

His mind filled with a vision of Alexa chasing his kids around, all wet from the tub. Warm memories pulled him in with a reminder of the family life he should be having right now and wasn't because of his workload. Having Alexa here felt so right.

It *was* right.

And so, he wasn't sending her back in the morning. In fact, he had to find a way to extend their window of time together. He not only needed her help with the children, but he also wanted her to stay for more *personal* reasons. The explosive chemistry they'd just discovered didn't come around often. Hell, he couldn't remember when he'd ever burned to have a particular woman this much. So much the craving filled his mind as well as his body.

The extension of their trip presented the perfect opportunity to follow that attraction to its ultimate destination.

Landing her directly into his bed.

Sunlight streamed through the window over the array of clothes laid out on the bed. So many clothes. Far more than she needed for a day or two.

Although as Alexa looked closer, she noticed the variety. It was as if whoever had shopped for her had planned for any contingency. Tan capris with a shabby chic blouse. A simple red cocktail dress. A sexy black bathing suit that looked far from nannylike and made her wonder who'd placed the order. At least there was a crocheted cover-up. And for this morning's breakfast...

She wore a silky sundress, floral with coral-tinted tulips in a watercolor print. Strappy gold sandals wrapped up and around her ankles. She scraped her hair back with a matching scarf that trailed down her back.

There was a whole other shopping bag that a quick peek told her held more clothes, underwear, a nightgown and a fabric cosmetics bag full of toiletries. Once upon a time, she'd taken these kinds of luxuries for granted, barely noticing when they appeared in her room or at a hotel.

These days she had a firm grasp on how hard she would have to work to pay for even one of these designer items. What a difference a year could make in a person's life. Yet, here she was again, dancing on the periphery of a world that had almost swallowed her whole.

Steeling her resolve to keep her values firmly in place, she strode from the bedroom into the sitting area where Seth was strapping the twins into the new, top-of–the-line double stroller.

He looked up and smiled. The power of his vibrant green eyes and dimples reached across the room, wrapping around her, enticing her to move closer into the circle of that happiness. A dangerous move. She had to step away, for her own peace of mind. She wasn't wired to leap into intimacy with a stranger.

A stranger who became more intriguing by the second.

Surely a billionaire who knew how to work a stroller couldn't be totally disconnected from everyday reality. That insight buoyed her, and inspired her. Actively learning more about him would help her on many levels. Knowing more about him was wise for her work.

For work, damn it, not because of this insane attraction.

"Are you ready?" he asked.

"Yes, I believe I am." She could do this. She could keep her professional face in place, while discovering if Seth Jansen harbored any more surprises in that hulking hot body of his.

"Glad the clothes fit. Although for breakfast with the twins, we might be better off draping ourselves in rain ponchos."

Before she could laugh or reply, his phone rang and

he held up a hand. "Hold on, I've got to take this. Work call coming in."

He started talking into his cell and grabbed his briefcase off the sofa. Opening the door, he gestured her ahead. She wheeled the stroller forward, out into the hall and toward the elevator.

The fabric slid sensuously against her skin with each step as she pushed the stroller into the elevator while Seth spoke on his phone to his partner…Rick… briefcase in his other hand. Each glide of the silky dress against her skin reminded her how vibrantly in tune her senses were this morning, and, as much as she wanted to credit the sunshine, she knew it was last night's kiss that had awakened something inside her.

Something that made professional goals tougher to keep in focus.

Two floors down, the doors slid open to admit an older couple dressed casually in sightseeing clothes that still shouted Armani and Prada. They fit right in with the rest of the clientele here. Except the woman carried a simple canvas bag with little handprints painted on it and signed in childlike handwriting. Stenciled along the top of the bag were the words Grandma's Angels. Alexa swallowed a lump of emotion as she counted at least eleven different scrawled signatures.

The husband leaned closer to his wife, whispering, pointing and smiling nostalgically. The wife knelt to pick up a tiny tennis shoe and passed it to Alexa. "You have a beautiful family."

Before Alexa could correct her, they reached the lobby and the couple exited. She glanced sheepishly toward Seth and found him staring at her with assessing eyes as he tucked away his phone. Her mouth went dry.

She grabbed the stroller, grateful for the support as the now increasingly predictable wobbly knees syndrome set in.

Ever aware of his gaze following her, she wheeled the twins from the elevator. She needed to get her thoughts in order ASAP. She was seconds away from meeting royalty for breakfast, pretty heady stuff even given her own upbringing. Seth was certainly coming through on his promise to introduce her to prestigious connections. Knowing the Medina family could be a serious boon to her fledgling business.

Although she was confused by a person who invited twin toddlers to a business breakfast at a restaurant with silk, antiques and a ceiling hand-painted with twenty-four karat gold.

The clink of silverware echoing from the room full of patrons, she didn't have to wonder for even a second which pair of diners to approach. A dark-haired, aristocratic man stood from a table set for six, nodding in their direction. A blonde woman sat beside him, a flower tucked behind her ear.

The wheels of the stroller glided smoothly along the tile floor as they passed a waiter carrying plates of crepes on his tray. Alexa stopped by their table.

Seth shook the man's hand. "Javier, I'd like you to meet—"

The man took her hand. "Alexa Randall. A pleasure to meet you," Javier said with only a hint of an accent. He motioned to the elegant woman beside him. "This is my wife, Victoria."

"Lovely to meet you." Victoria smiled welcomingly, while tucking her fingers into the crook of her husband's arm. He covered her hand automatically with a possessive and affectionate air.

Good God, this place was chock full of couples swimming in marital bliss. First the elderly couple in the elevator. Now her dining companions for breakfast. She didn't even dare look at the couple feeding each other bits of melon at the table next to them.

The numbers of fawning couples here defied national divorce statistics. Although, now that she thought about it, she and Seth had enough breakups to even out the scales.

Leaning into the stroller, Victoria grinned at the twins and spun a rattle attached to the tray. "Would you mind if I held one of these sweethearts?"

Seth pulled back the stroller canopy. "Sure, this is Owen—" he picked up his son "—and this is Olivia."

As Victoria reached down, the little girl stretched her arms up toward Alexa instead. Alexa's heart squeezed in response. So much so, it scared her a little. These babies were quickly working their way into her affection. Victoria eased back gracefully and left Alexa to settle the baby girl into her high chair beside her brother's. The adults took their seats and placed their orders, so far, with no mishaps.

As the waitress placed each person's dish on the table, Victoria spread her linen napkin across her lap. "I told Javier he really put you on the spot insisting you bring along babies, but the twins are total dolls." She tickled Olivia's chin. "Hopefully you'll warm up to me, sweetie, so I can entertain you while Alexa eats her breakfast, too."

"I think I can manage, but thank you." She reached past her smoked salmon bagel for her goblet of juice.

How well did this woman and her husband already know Seth? What kind of information might she learn during this breakfast about Seth and his possible contacts?

While Javier detailed the must-see sights in St. Augustine, Olivia and Owen fed themselves fruit—which scared Alexa to her last frazzled nerve as she watched to be sure strawberries stayed on Olivia's tray but not Owen's.

Seth shoveled in steak and eggs, spooning oatmeal into the twins' mouths, while holding a conversation. She was in awe.

And a little intimidated.

She'd almost flooded the floor last night during their bath. If he hadn't shown up early, she wasn't sure how she would have wrestled them both into clothes. Whenever she thought she'd moved everything dangerous out of their reach...

Oh, God...

She lunged for Olivia just as Seth smoothly pulled the salt shaker from her grasp. Her pulse rate doubled at the near miss with catastrophe. So much for using this breakfast to learn more about Seth from the Cortez couple. She would be lucky to make it through the meal with her sanity intact.

Victoria rested her knife at the top of her plate of half-eaten eggs Benedict. "I hope he's treating you to some vacation fun after all these stodgy business meetings are over."

"Pardon?" Alexa struggled to keep track of the twins and the conversation in the middle of a business meeting and a dining room full of tourists.

Glasses and silverware clinked and clattered. Waiters

angled past with loaded trays as people fueled up for the day ahead.

Victoria swiped her mouth with the linen napkin. "You deserve some pampering for watching the kids solo here at the hotel during the day."

"I'm helping out with temporary nanny detail."

Leaning closer, Victoria whispered, "It's obvious he doesn't look at you like a nanny."

She couldn't exactly deny that since she was likely searing him with her own glances, too. "Honestly we don't know each other that well."

Victoria waved away her comment, her wedding rings refracting light from the chandelier. "The length of time doesn't always matter when it comes to the heart. I knew right away Javier was the one." She smiled affectionately at her new husband, who was deep in conversation with Seth. "It took us a while to find our way to each other, but if I'd listened to my heart right off, we could have been saved so many months of grief."

"It's a business arrangement," she said simply, hoping if she repeated it enough she could maintain her objectivity. "Only business."

"Of course," Victoria conceded, but her smile didn't dim. "I'm sorry. I didn't mean to be nosy. It's just that given what I understand from Javier, Seth has been a workaholic since his divorce. He hasn't had time for relationships."

"There's nothing to apologize for." Alexa knew full well she and Seth were sending out mixed signals. As much as she'd been determined to keep things professional with Seth the businessman, she found herself drawn to Seth the father. A man so tender with his children. At ease with a baby stroller. As adept at flying a spoonful of oatmeal into a child's mouth as he was at piloting a plane through the sky.

These surprise insights proved a potent attraction, especially after living with her own distant father and then the way her ex had checked out on her.

Victoria's voice pulled Alexa out of her musings.

"Honestly, my thoughts may be selfish. I was thinking ahead that if Javier and Seth settle on a contract, then I was hoping we would get to see more of each other. As much as I adore my husband, his world is narrow and he's suspicious of expanding the circle. I'm always grateful for some girl time."

"That would be lovely, thank you." Alexa understood perfectly about lonely inner circles, too much so. She felt a twinge of guilt over her thoughts about using the Cortezes for contacts.

All her life she'd been warned about gold diggers. She'd always known the chances of someone seeing through the money to love her for herself was slim. And still she'd made a royal mess. She didn't want to let the Cortez money and their Medina connections blind her to who they really were.

"I mean it. And regardless of how much time we spend visiting, let's enjoy the day…let's have fun."

Fun? She should be home, at work. She took a deep breath. This situation would help her at work. Or she hoped so.

She couldn't ignore the fact that her wish to stay right here was increasing by the second. "I appreciate how helpful you've been here at breakfast. The twins are my responsibility. We're going sightseeing with the stroller, maybe do a little shopping."

"Perfect," Victoria declared. "I'm at loose ends. I

love a good walk and shopping. And after that, we can wear them out at the pool."

Alexa did have a swimsuit and she had absolutely no reason not to take Victoria up on her generous offer. No reason other than a deep-seated fear of allowing herself to be tempted back into a world she'd been determined to leave behind. A way of life embraced by Seth and his precious children. Her eyes were drawn back to the twins.

Just as Owen wrapped his fist around one of his sister's strawberries—a food he was allergic to.

Panic gripped Alexa as she saw the baby's lightning fast intent to gobble the forbidden fruit. "No! Owen, don't eat that."

Lurching toward him, she grabbed his chubby wrist just before his hand reached his mouth. His face scrunched into utter dejection as his tiny world crumbled over the lost treat. Alexa winced a second ahead of his piercing scream. Seth leaned in to soothe the temper tantrum. Before Alexa could even form the words of warning...

Olivia flipped the bowl of oatmeal straight into Javier Cortez's lap.

Five

The cosmos must have been holding a serious grudge against him because the sight of Alexa in a bathing suit sucker-punched him clean through.

Seth stopped short by the poolside bar outside the hotel and allowed himself a moment to soak in the sunlit view, a welcome pleasure after a tense work day that had started with his kid dumping oatmeal in a prospective customer's lap. Thank goodness Javier Cortez had insisted it didn't matter.

And Alexa had acted fast by scooping up both twins and taking them away for the day.

Now, she looked anything but maternal as she rubbed sunscreen down her arms, laughing at something Victoria said. The twins slept in a playpen under the shade of a small open cabana. Only a half dozen others had stayed this late in the day—a young couple drinking wine in the hot tub and a family playing with a beach ball in the shallow end.

His attention stayed fully focused on the goddess in black Lycra.

He should be celebrating the success of his day's meeting. Javier wanted him to tour the landing strip at the king's private island off the coast of St. Augustine. Their time here was done. The king's island even came equipped with a top-notch nanny for the twins, a nanny the king kept on staff for his grandchildren's visits.

And yet, Seth was all the more determined than ever to keep Alexa with him, to win her over, to seduce her into his bed again and again until he worked this tenacious attraction out of their systems. He hadn't yet attained that goal but was determined to keep her around until he succeeded.

The black bathing suit was more modest than the strings other women wore that barely held in the essentials. Still, there was no denying her sensuality. Halter neckline, plunging deeply until the top of her belly button ring showed.

A simple gold hoop.

His hands itched to grasp her hips and slide his fingers along the edges, slipping inside to feel the satiny slickness he knew waited right there. For him.

Splashing from the deep end snapped him back to reality. Damn, he seriously needed to rein in those kinds of thoughts out here in public. Even when they were alone. He needed to be patient. He didn't want to spook her into bailing on this time they had together.

He thought back to how fast she'd retreated after their kiss. She'd been undeniably as turned on as he was and yet, she'd avoided him that morning as they'd prepared for the day. Although he thought he sensed a bit of softening in her stance as the day wore on. At breakfast he'd thought he caught her eyes lingering on him more than once. He could see the memory of their kiss written in her eyes as she stared at him with a mixture of confusion and attraction.

Shoving away from the bar, Seth strode alongside the pool toward Alexa. "Good afternoon, ladies."

Jolted, she looked over at him. Her eyes widened and he could have sworn goose bumps of awareness rose along her arms. She yanked her crocheted cover-up off the glass-topped table and shrugged into it almost fast enough to hide her breasts beading with arousal. His own body throbbed in response, his hands aching to cradle each creamy globe in his palms.

"Seth, I didn't expect you back this early."

Out of the corner of his eyes, he saw Victoria gather her beach bag. "Since you're done for the day, I take it my husband's free, so if you'll both excuse me…"

The woman made a smooth—and timely—exit.

Seth sank down into her vacated lounger beside Alexa as a teenager cannonballed into the deep end. "Did you and the babies have a good afternoon?"

"No problems or I would have called you. I wrote down everything the children ate and when they went to sleep. The pool time wore them out." She toyed with the tie on her cover up—right between her breasts.

He forced his gaze to stay on her face. "I want you to extend your time with us for a couple more days."

Her jaw went slack with surprise before she swallowed hard. "You want me to stay with you and the children?"

"Precisely."

"My business is a small operation—"

"What about your partner?"

"I can't dump everything on her indefinitely and still meet our obligations."

His point exactly as for why hers wasn't the company for Jansen Jets—hers wasn't large enough and didn't have adequate backup resources. He leaned forward, elbows resting on his knees. "I thought you were cleaning my plane to meet with me."

"That certainly was my intent—and to impress you with A-1's work." She hugged her legs. "But I do clean other aircraft in addition to my obligations to office work."

"That doesn't leave much time for a private life." Late day sun beating down on his head, he shrugged out of his suit jacket and draped it over the back of the lounger. He loosened his tie. God, he hated the constraining things.

"I'm investing in my future."

"I understand completely." His eyes gravitated toward his children, still sleeping peacefully in the playpen—Olivia on her tummy with her diapered butt up in the air, Owen on his back with his arms flung wide.

"You've achieved your goals. That's admirable. I'm working on my dream now." Determination coated each word as fully as the sunscreen covered her bared skin.

He *really* didn't need to be thinking about her exposed body right now.

Already, he was on the edge of a new deal with Javier Cortez to supply charter jets for the royal Medinas. That huge boon would take his company to the next level and free him up to set up an entire volunteer, nonprofit foundation devoted to search and rescue operations. His first love, what had drawn him into flying in the first place. That love of flying had helped him develop and patent the airport security device that had made him a mint. Once he took his business to the next level, funding and overstretched government budgets wouldn't be an issue...

So damn close to achieving all his business dreams.

Yet, still he was restless. "Let's forget arguing about tomorrow and business. We can hash that out later. Right now, I'm off the clock. I want to make the most of our time left in St. Augustine tonight."

"What exactly did you have in mind?" She eyed him suspiciously.

Had he imagined her softening on the all-business stance? There was only one way to find out.

Standing, he snagged his suit coat. "We're going to spend the evening out."

"With twins? Don't you think breakfast was pushing our luck?"

He grinned, scooping up his groggy daughter. "Trust me. I can handle this."

"All right, if you're sure."

"Absolutely." He palmed his daughter's back as she wriggled in his arms and tugged at his collar. "Wait until you see what I have planned. You'll want to dress comfortably, though. And we should probably pack extra clothes for the kids in case they get dirty."

Alexa pulled up alongside him, Owen in her arms. Seth reached for the door inside—

Until her gasp stopped him short.

"Did you forget something?" he asked.

When Alexa didn't answer, he glanced and found her

staring back at him with horror. What the hell? Except as she raised a shaking hand to point, he realized she wasn't looking at him. Her attention was focused fully on Olivia.

More precisely, on Olivia's bulging left nostril.

Sitting on the edge of the hotel sofa in their suite, Alexa struggled to contain the squirming little girl in her lap while pushing back the welling panic. The whole ride up in the elevator had been crazy, with Seth attempting to check his daughter's nose and the child growing more agitated by the second.

How in the world had Olivia wedged something up her nostril? More importantly, *what* had she shoved into there?

Alexa winced at the baby's bulging left nostril. She hadn't taken her eyes off Olivia for a second during their time at the pool—except when Olivia had been sleeping. Had she woken up? Found something in the playpen? Perhaps something blew inside the pen with her?

Panic gripped her. What the hell had she been thinking, allowing herself to believe she could care for these two precious children? She willed herself to stop shaking and deal with the crisis at hand.

Seth knelt in front of her, trying to grasp his daughter's head between his palms. "I can get this out if you will just hold her still long enough for me to push my thumb down the outside of her nose."

"Believe me, I'm trying my best." Alexa's heart pumped as hard and fast as Olivia's feet as the little girl screamed, kicking her father in the stomach. Her face turned red; her skin beaded with sweat from hysteria.

Sinking back on his haunches, Seth looked around their suite. "Is there any pepper left from last night's dinner?"

"Housekeeping cleared away everything. Oh, God, I am so sorry. I don't know how this happened—"

A crash echoed through the room.

Alexa looked at Seth, her panic mirrored in his eyes. "Owen!"

They both shot to their feet just as a pitiful wail drifted from behind the velvet sofa. Holding Olivia around the waist, Alexa ran fast on Seth's heels, only to slam against his back when he stopped short.

Owen sat on the floor, blessedly unharmed, just angry. His "tower"—which consisted of a chair, a pillow and the ice bucket—now lay on its side by the television. Handprints all over the flat screen testified to his attempt to turn on the TV by himself.

Seth knelt beside his son, running his hands along the toddler's arms and legs. "Are you okay, buddy? You know you're not supposed to climb like that." His thumb brushed over his son's forehead, along the eyebrow that still carried a scar from past stitches. "Be careful."

Picking up Owen, Seth held him close for a second, a sigh of relief racking through his body so visibly Alexa almost melted into the floor with sympathy. God, this big manly guy who plowed through life and through the skies alone had the most amazing way of connecting with his kids.

What would it have been like to grow up with a father like him? A dad so very present in his children's lives?

Standing, Seth said, "I'm going to have to take Olivia to the emergency room. Swap kids with me. You can stay here with Owen."

"You still trust me?"

"Of course," he responded automatically even though his mouth had gone tight. With frustration? Fear?

Or anger?

He leaned toward her. Olivia let out a high-pitched shriek and locked her arms tighter around Alexa's neck, turning her face frantically from her father.

Seth frowned. "It's okay, kiddo. It's just me."

Patting Olivia's back, Alexa swayed soothingly from side to side. "She must think you're going to pinch her nose again."

"Well, we don't have much choice here. I need to take her in." He set down Owen and clasped his daughter.

Olivia's cries cranked up to earsplitting wails, which upset her brother who started sobbing on the floor. If Olivia kept gasping would whatever was in her nose get sucked in? And then where would it go? Into a lung? The possibilities were horrifying. This parenting thing was not for the faint of heart.

"Seth, let me hold her rather than risk her becoming even more hysterical." She cradled the little girl's head, blond curls looping around Alexa's fingers as surely as the child was sliding into Alexa's heart. "You and I can go to the emergency room and take both kids."

Plowing a hand through his hair, Seth looked around the suite again as if searching for other options. Finally he nodded and picked up his son. "That's probably for the best. We just have to get a car." He grabbed the room phone and dialed the hotel operator. "Seth Jansen here. We need transportation to the nearest E.R. waiting for us. We're headed to the elevator now."

She jammed her feet into the flip-flops she'd worn to the pool, grateful she'd at least had time to change out of her swimsuit, and followed Seth out into the hall. The elevator opened immediately—thank God—and they plunged inside the empty compartment. He jostled his restless son while she made *shhh, shhh, shhh* soothing sounds for Olivia, who was now hiccupping. But at least the little girl wasn't crying.

The floors dinged by, but not fast enough. The doors parted and the elderly couple they'd seen on their way down to breakfast stepped inside.

Dressed to the nines in jewels and evening wear, the woman wasn't carrying her canvas bag made by her grandchildren, but she still radiated a grandma air. She leaned toward Olivia and crooned, "What's the matter, sweetie? Why the tears?"

Lines of strain and worry pulled tighter at the corners of Seth's mouth. "She shoved something up her nose," he said curtly, his gaze locked in on the elevator numbers as if willing the car to move faster. "We're headed to the E.R."

As if sensing her dad's intent, Olivia pressed her face into Alexa's neck.

The grandmother looked back at her husband and winked knowingly. The older gentleman, dressed in a tuxedo, reached past Alexa so quickly she didn't have time to think.

He tugged Olivia's ear. "What's that back there behind your ear, little one?" His hand came back around with a gold cuff link in his palm. "Was that in your ear?"

Olivia peeked around to see and like lightning, the grandmother reached past and swiped her finger down Olivia's nose. A white button shot out and into the woman's hand. She held it up to Seth's shirt. A perfect match. They hadn't even noticed he was missing one from near his neck.

Surprise stamped on his handsome face, Seth stuffed the button into his pocket. "She must have pulled it off when I picked her up by the pool."

Alexa gasped in awe at how easily the couple had handled mining the button from Olivia's nose. "How did you two manage that so smoothly?"

The grandpa straightened his tuxedo bow tie. "Lots of practice. You two will get the knack before you know it."

In a swirl of diamonds and expensive perfume, the couple swept out of the elevator, leaving Alexa and Seth inside. The doors slid closed again. She sagged back against the brass rail. Relief left her weak-kneed all the way back to the penthouse floor while Seth called downstairs on his cell to cancel their ride to the E.R.

Stopping just outside their door, he tucked his phone in his pocket and slid a hand behind her neck. "Thank you."

"For what? I feel like I've let you down." The emotions and worry after the scare with Olivia had left her spinning. She could only imagine how he must feel.

"Thank you for being here. Chasing these two is more challenging than flying a plane through a thunderstorm." He scrubbed a hand over his jaw. "My family tells me I'm not too good at asking for help. But I gotta admit having an extra set of hands and eyes around made things easier just now."

His emerald-green gaze warmed her along with his words. Given her history with men, the whole trust notion was tough for her. But right now, she so desperately wanted to believe in the sincerity she saw in his eyes. She felt appreciated. Valued as a person.

Giving that much control to another person scared her spitless. "You're welcome."

She thought for a moment he was going to kiss her again. Her lips tingled at the prospect. But then he glanced at the two children and eased back. "Let's get the diaper bag so we can move forward with our night out on the town."

Blinking fast, she stood stock-still for a second, barely registering his words. They still had a whole night ahead of them? She was wrung out, as if she'd run an emotional marathon. With her defenses in the negative numbers, an evening out with Seth and his children was too tantalizing, too tempting a prospect. Hell, the man himself was too tempting. Not that she had the choice of opting out.

She just really hoped the evening sucked.

The evening hadn't sucked.

In fact, Seth had followed through with the perfect plans so far, starting off with a gourmet picnic at a park near a seventeenth century fort by the harbor. The children had toddled around, eaten their fill and gotten dirty. So precious and perfect and far more normal than she would have expected.

Then Seth had chartered a carriage ride through the historic district at sundown. Olivia and Owen had squealed with delight over the horse. And the last part of the outing hadn't ended in a half hour as she'd expected.

Once the kids' bedtime arrived, Seth had simply paid the driver to continue down the waterside road while the children slept in their laps. The *clop, clop, clop* of the Belgian draft's hooves lulled Alexa as she cuddled the sweet weight of Owen sleeping in her arms.

The night was more than Cinderella-perfect. Cinderella only had the prospect of happily ever after. For tonight, Alexa had experienced the magic of being a part of a real family during this outing with Seth and his children.

Although Cinderella's driver likely wasn't sporting ear buds for an iPod. Alexa appreciated the privacy it offered as she didn't have to worry about him eavesdropping.

Being a part of a family taking a magical moonlit carriage ride presented a tableau she'd dreamed about. The way Olivia nestled so trustingly against her father's chest. The obvious affection between him and his children during their picnic. He'd built a relationship with them, complete with familiar games and songs and love.

But even as she joined in this family game for now, she couldn't lose sight of her real role here. Or the fact that Seth Jansen was a sharp businessman, known for his drive for perfection and no-nonsense ways.

She knew he wanted her. Could he be devious enough to use his children to keep her here? She thought of earlier, by the pool, how he'd focused all that intensity on her. His eyes had stroked over her, hot and hungry.

Exciting.

There'd been a time when she couldn't show her body in a bathing suit—for fear people would find out her secret, because of her own hang-ups. She'd worked past that. She'd come to peace with herself. But as her thoughts drifted toward the possibility of intimacy with another person, she faced the reality of sharing that secret part of herself, to explain why she had such extensive stretch marks in spite of never having had a child.

Even though she'd found resolution inside, it wasn't something she enjoyed revisiting.

She rested her chin on Owen's head, Seth sitting across from her holding Olivia. "How did your business meeting go?"

"We're moving forward, closer to a deal than before. My gut tells me there's a real possibility I can land this one."

"If he hasn't ended the negotiations, that's got to be a positive sign." She settled into the professional discussion, thinking of how far she'd come from her teenage years of insecurity.

"That's my take." He nodded, then something shifted in his eyes. "It appeared you had fun with Victoria today."

More memories of his interest at the pool, of his kiss last night steamed through her as tangibly as the heat rising from the paved road. A cooling breeze rolled off the harbor and caressed her shoulders, lifting her hair the way his fingers had played through the strands.

Her hand lifted to swipe back a lock from her face. "I feel guilty calling this work when it really has been more of a vacation."

"You've had twins to watch over. That's hardly a holiday."

"I've had a lot of help from you and Victoria." The carriage driver tugged the reins at a stop sign, a towering adobe church on the corner. "Not that any of us could stop that oatmeal incident."

He chuckled softly. "Thank goodness Javier's more laid back than I would have given him credit for."

"It was gracious of him to acknowledge that the breakfast with toddlers was his idea." She shuffled Owen into a more comfortable position as the baby settled deeper into sleep. "What made you think of taking a carriage ride to help the twins wind down?"

"I spent so much time outdoors growing up." He patted his daughter's back softly. "I try to give that to my kids when I can."

"Well, this was a great idea…" The moonlight played across the water rippling in the harbor. "The night air, the gorgeous scenery, the water, it's been quite a break for me, too."

"I never get tired of the year-round good weather here." As he sat across from her, he propped a foot beside her on the seat.

"What about January through March?" She shivered melodramatically. "The cold wind off the water is biting."

His laugh rode the ocean breeze as he opened up more as the evening wore on. "You've obviously never visited North Dakota. My uncle would get icicles in his beard in the winter."

"No kidding?"

"No kidding." He scratched his chin as if caught in the memories. "My cousins and I still went outside, no matter how far the temperature dropped, but it's a lot easier here when it doesn't take a half hour to pull on so many layers of clothes."

"What did you like to do in North Dakota?" she asked, hungry for deeper peeks into this intriguing man.

"Typical stuff, snowmobiling, hiking, horseback

riding on the farm. Then I discovered flying..." He shrugged. "And here I am now."

Yet there was so much more to him than that, this man who'd come from a North Dakota farm and made billions off his interest in airplanes.

The carriage shocks squeaked as the large wheels rolled along a brick side-road. How was it she felt tipsy when she hadn't even had so much as a sip of alcohol?

He nudged the side of her leg with his foot. "What about you? What did you want to do when you were a kid?"

"Art history, remember?" she said evasively.

"Why art history?"

"An obsession with creating beauty, I guess."

And now they were dancing a little too close to uncomfortable territory from her past. She pointed to the old-fashioned sailboat anchored near the shore with the sounds of a party carrying across the water. "What's up with that?"

He hesitated for a moment as if he understood full well she was trying to redirect the conversation. "It's a pirate ship. The *Black Raven*. They do everything from kids' parties to the more adult sort." He gestured toward a couple in buccaneer and maid costumes strolling down the sidewalk. "Then there are regular bar hours. People come in costume. I thought about having a party for the kids there someday—during regular hours, of course."

"I can envision you in a Jack Sparrow-style pirate shirt so you wouldn't have to tug at your tie all the time."

"You've noticed that?"

She shrugged, staying silent.

"There are lots of things I hope to teach my kids." He pointed toward the sky. "Like showing them the Big Dipper there. Or my favorite constellation, Orion's belt. See the orange-looking star along the strand? That's Betelgeuse, a red star. There's nothing like charting the sky."

"Sounds like you have a pirate's soul. If you'd been born before airplanes…"

"Star navigation can be helpful if you're lost," he pointed out. "Betelgeuse saved my ass from getting lost more than once when the navigational instruments went on the fritz during a search."

She thought back to her research on him from when she'd put together her proposal. "You started your company doing search and rescue."

"I'm still active in that arena."

"Really?" Why hadn't she seen information about that kind of work? That could have been useful in her proposal. She wanted to kick herself for falling short. "I didn't realize that."

"SAR—search and rescue—was my first love. Still is," he said with undeniable fire.

"Then why do you do the corporate charter gig?" The image of Seth Jansen was more confusing with each new revelation. She hadn't expected so many layers, so much depth.

"Search and rescue doesn't pay well. So the bigger my business…"

"The more good you can do." And just that fast the pieces came together, the billionaire, the father, the philanthropist. And on top of everything he was hot?

God, she was in serious deep water here.

His gaze slid to hers, held and heated. In a smooth

move, he shifted off the seat across from her to sit beside her. The scent of his crisp aftershave teased her nose, while his hulking magnetism drew her. Before she could think, she swayed toward him.

They still held both sleeping children, so nothing could or would happen. But the connection between them was tangible. His eyes invited her to lean against him and his arm slid around her shoulders, tucking her closer as the carriage rolled on.

How far did she want to take this? She hadn't forgotten his request that she extend her stay, even if he hadn't brought it up again. Then there was the whole tangle of her wanting to work for him...

And there were these two beautiful children who obviously came first with him, as they should. She understood how deeply a child could be affected by their growing up years. She carried the scars of her own childhood, complete with fears about opening herself to another relationship, making herself vulnerable to a man by baring her secrets as well as her body.

The carriage jerked to a halt outside their hotel, and her time to decide what to do next came to an end.

Seth set his iPod in the hotel's docking station and cued up the twins' favorite Mozart for tots music. The babies had been too groggy for baths after the carriage ride, so he and Alexa had just tucked them into their cribs, each wearing a fresh diaper and T-shirt.

Leaving him alone with Alexa—and completely awake.

Their evening together had given him an opportunity to learn more about her, the person, rather than the businesswoman. Guilt tweaked his conscience. She

had a life and a company and a tender heart. She also
had some misguided notion she could persuade him
to sign a contract with her cleaning service. He'd told
her otherwise, but he suspected she believed she could
change his mind.

He needed to clear that up now, before things went
further.

While he would do anything for his kids, he had
other options for their care now and he couldn't deny
the truth. He was keeping her here because he wanted
to sleep with her, now, away from Charleston, in a way
that wouldn't tangle their lives up with each other.
Because, damn it all, no matter how much he wanted
her in his bed, he didn't have the time or inclination to
start a full out relationship. He would not, under any
circumstances put his children through the upheaval of
another inevitable breakup.

He plowed his fingers through his hair. He was left
with no choice. He had to come clean with Alexa. He
owed it to her. If for no other reason than because of
the way she'd been so patient with his children, more
than just watching over them, she'd played with them.

Rolled a ball.

Kissed a minor boo-boo.

Wiped away pudding smudges from their faces.

Rested her cheek on a sleeping baby's head with such
genuine affection while they rode in the carriage like
an honest to God family.

A dark cloud mushroomed inside him. He pivoted
toward the living room—and found her waiting in the
open doorway. She still wore the tan capris and flowing
blouse she'd had on for their picnic, except her feet
were bare.

Her toes curled into the carpet. "Earlier tonight, you mentioned extending our stay. What was that all about?"

He should be rejoicing. He had achieved exactly what he wanted in enticing her to stay.

Yet now was his time to man-up and tell her the whole story. "There's been a change in plans. I'm not returning to Charleston in the morning."

"You're staying here?" Her forehead crinkled in confusion.

He glanced back at his kids, concerned with waking them, and guided Alexa into the living area, closing the bedroom door behind him.

"Not exactly." He steered her to the blue velvet sofa and sat beside her. "Tomorrow, Javier and I are moving negotiations to the king's island to peruse his landing strip and discuss possibilities for increasing security measures."

"That's great news for you." She smiled with genuine pleasure.

Her obvious—unselfish—happiness over his success kicked his guilt into high gear. "I need to be up-front with you."

"Okay—" her eyes went wary "—I'm listening."

"I want you to come with me to the island." He tucked a knuckle under her chin, brushed his mouth over hers. The connection deepened, crackled with need. "Not because of business or the kids. But because I want *you*. I want *this*."

He hesitated. "And before you ask, I do still intend to introduce you to the contacts just like I promised on day one. And I will listen to your business proposal and give you advice. But that's all I can offer."

Small consolation to his burning conscience right

now. He truly wished he could do more for her and for her business.

Realization dawned in her eyes, her face paling. "I'm not going to land the Jansen Jets contract, no matter what I say."

"I'm afraid not. Your company is simply not large enough. I'm sorry."

She gnawed her plump bottom lip, then braced her shoulders. "You don't have to apologize. You told me as much that first day, and I just didn't want to hear you."

"The way your service is growing shows promise, and if this had been a year from now, the answer might have been different." That made him wonder what it would have been like to meet her a year from now, when his kids were older and the sting of his divorce had lessened.

"Then I go home now."

Was that anger or regret he saw chasing across her expression? It looked enough like the latter that he wasn't going to miss the opportunity to press what little advantage he had. "Or you could go with me to the island. Just for the weekend."

Her lips pressed tightly, thinning. "You may always get weekends free, but Bethany and I trade off every other one. I've already taken two days off work in the hope of a business proposition you never intended to fulfill. I can't keep imposing on her indefinitely."

"I meant what I said. I do intend to make good on introducing you to new connections and helping you beef up your presentation. Damn it, I'm trying hard to be honest with you." He reached to loosen his tie and then realized he wasn't wearing it anymore. "I'll pay the difference you need to hire temporary help while you're away—"

Her eyes went wide with horror. "You've already paid me enough. It's not about the money."

"Take it anyway. Consider it an exchange for your help with the kids. And I do need your help."

"You want me to stay for the twins?" She crossed her arms defensively.

"It's not that simple. I can't untangle my kids from what's going on between us. So yeah, they factor into this decision." They had to factor into every decision he made. "My children like you. That counts for a lot. They've seen too much upheaval in their lives already. I try to give them as much stability as I can."

"They've only known me for a couple of days and then I'll be gone." Her fingers dug into her elbows.

She had a point there. The thought of them growing too attached…

Shaking his head, he refocused. His plan for the weekend was solid. Second-guessing himself would only derail things. He loosened her grip and held her soft hands in his. "I like how happy Owen and Olivia are with you."

"I adore them, too." Obvious affection tinged her words, along with regret. "But even if I agree to this crazy proposition of yours, I'll be leaving their lives when we all go home."

"Maybe. Maybe not." Where had that come from? Only seconds ago he'd been thinking about how he needed to have an affair now because indulging in more once they returned home wasn't an option.

Was it?

She tugged her hands from his. "I'm not ready for

any kind of relationship, and I'm still not happy about the business end of things between us."

He should be rejoicing at those words. Should be. He cradled her face in his palm. "Then consider having a fling with me."

"A fling?" She gnawed her bottom lip slowly as she repeated the word. "Fling? No attachment or expectations. Just pure indulgence in each other?"

Already her suggestive words sent a bolt of lust straight to his groin. If she could seduce him this thoroughly with just a few words, what more did she hold in store with her hands, her body?

"That's the idea," he growled softly in agreement. "We pick up where we left off last night at dinner."

So he waited for her decision, the outcome more important than it should have been for someone of such brief acquaintance. But then she smiled, not full out, just a hint of possibility.

She reached, skimming her fingers down the front of his chest lightly as if still making up her mind. The feel of her featherlight touch made his erection impossibly harder.

Her hand stopped just shy of his belt, her eyes assessing, yet still holding the briefest hint of reservation. "For how long?"

He clasped her hand and brought her wrist to his mouth. Her pulse leaped under his kiss.

"For the weekend." Or more. He wasn't sure of a hell of a lot right now. But he was certain of one thing. He wanted Alexa. "Starting now."

Six

Alexa leaned into the restrained strength of Seth's touch. He was such a giant of a man with amazing control. She'd been aching for the feel of his hands on her skin since she'd first seen him. Yes, she was angry over the doused hopes of signing a contract with his company. However, in other ways, she was relieved. The end of their business acquaintance freed her to pursue the attraction between them.

As much as she wanted to attribute the power of her desire to months of abstinence, she knew she hadn't felt anything near this compulsion for other attractive men who'd crossed her path. She wanted him, deeply, ached to have him with such a craving it was all she could do not to fling herself onto him.

Even in her spoiled princess days, she'd guarded her body closely. She'd only slept with two men before her husband and no one since. Each relationship had come after months of dating. This was so out of character for her, which emphasized the tenacious attraction all the more.

The prospect of a no-strings affair with Seth, especially now that she wasn't trying to win a contract with him, was more temptation than she could resist.

She angled her face into his hard hand, turning to press a kiss into his palm. A primitive growl of desire rumbled from him in response, stirring and stoking molten pleasure deep in her belly.

Without moving his hand from her face, he leaned to kiss her bared neck. The glide of his mouth sent delicious shivers down her spine. Her head lolled back to give him fuller access.

He swept her hair aside with a large confident hand that skimmed down to palm her waist. Nipping, kissing, his mouth traced along her throbbing pulse. His chin nudged aside one shoulder of her blouse, his late-day beard raspy and arousing against her flushed skin.

His body hummed with restraint. Straining tendons along his neck let her know just how much it cost him to go slowly. His meticulous attention to detail sent a fresh shiver of anticipation through her.

She grabbed his shirt, her fist twisting in the warm cotton as she hauled him closer, urged him on. He shot to his feet and scooped her into his arms. Her fingers linked behind his neck as she steadied herself against his chest. Part of her warned that she should stop, now; but an even more insistent part of her urged her to see this through. Then maybe she would be free of the frenetic lure of this man. She could get back to the carefully planned, safe life she'd built for herself.

Seth angled sideways through the door into the spare room. Gauzy curtains hung from rings around the wrought-iron canopy frame overhead. He lowered her gently into the poofy white spread. Stepping back, he began unbuttoning his shirt while she watched— not that he seemed the least concerned with her gaze clinging to him.

In fact, he appeared all the more aroused by her appreciation. He shrugged off the shirt and unbuckled his belt, the low lighting from the bedside lamp casting a warm glow over his bared flesh.

One long zip later... Oh, yeah, he was most definitely as turned on as she was. The rigid length of his arousal reached up his rock solid abs. Golden hair sprinkled along his defined chest. He was a sculpted god of a man, and for tonight, he was all hers...

But as she devoured him with her eyes, unease skittered up her spine at the prospect of turning the tables. While she'd conquered the eating disorder of her teenage years, her body still carried marks and signs of how close she'd come to dying.

Twisting sideways, she reached to turn off the lamp and prayed he wouldn't argue. She truly didn't want to have this discussion right now. *Click.* The room went dark then shadowy as her eyes adjusted to the moonlight streaming through the sheers on the window, the thicker brocade curtains pulled back.

She waited and thank God, Seth stayed silent. Brows pinching together, his head tilting to the side offered the only signs he'd registered her turning off the light.

Swallowing the patter of nerves, she sat up and swept her loose shirt upward and over her head. As she shook her hair free, he kicked aside his pants and leaned over her, angling her back to recline against the piled pillows. His hand fell to the top button on her capris. Up close, she could see the question in his eyes as he waited for her consent.

Arching upward, she slid her fingers into his hair and tugged his mouth toward hers. The feel of him was becoming familiar as they deepened contact, her lips parting, opening, welcoming him. Losing herself in the kiss, she barely registered his deft work pushing aside her pants and freeing the front clasp of her bra.

The cool air contrasted with the warmth of his hard muscled body. Tension built inside her, a need to take this farther, faster. She tugged at Seth's shoulders, whispering her need, her desires, but he wouldn't be rushed.

He nipped, licked, laved his way down her neck and to her breasts, drawing on her tightening nipples with the perfect mixture of tongue and tug. Her fingernails grazed down his back, tendons and muscles flexing under her stroke in response.

The glide of his hand between them sent her stomach muscles tensing. He slowed, pausing to flick her belly button ring. "This drove me insane when I saw it earlier, exposed by that sexy deep V of your bathing suit. Ever since, all I could think of was touching it. Touching you."

"Then I like the way you think," she whispered, then gasped.

His tender torment continued until her head thrashed along the deep downy pillow. She hooked her leg around his, bringing his stony thigh to rest against her aching core. Rocking against him only made her more frustrated, liquid longing pulsing through her veins and flushing her skin.

The air conditioner swirled the scents of his aftershave, her shampoo and their desire into a perfume of lust, intoxicating her with each gasping breath. He angled off her, and she moaned her frustration.

"Shh." He pressed a finger to her mouth. "Only for a second."

His hand dipped into a drawer in the bedside table. He came back with a box of condoms. Thank heaven, someone had the foresight to plan ahead. She couldn't even bring herself to condemn him for assuming this could happen...because here they were, the only place she wanted to be at the moment.

Then the thick pressure of him between her thighs scattered any other thoughts as he pushed inside her. Large and stretching and more than she'd expected. She hooked her legs around his waist, opening for him, welcoming him and the sensation of having him fully inside her.

Smoothly, he rolled to his back while their bodies stayed connected. She lay sprawled on top of him. Bowing upward, she straddled him, taking him impossibly deeper. His eyes flamed as he watched her with the same intensity she knew she'd lavished on him when he'd undressed for her. He gripped her waist, and she rolled her hips against him.

Her head flung back at the pure sensation, the perfect angle as he nudged against the circle of sensitivity hidden inside her. And again, he moved, thrusting, pumping, taking her need to a whole new level of frenzy until she raked her nails down his chest, desperate for completion. She didn't know herself, this out of control woman all but screaming for release. She'd thought she knew her body and the pleasures to be found in bed. But nothing came close to this…this fiery tingle along her every nerve.

Then they were flipping position again and he was on top of her, pumping faster, the head of his arousal tormenting that special spot inside her again and again until…

Sensation imploded, sparks of white light dotting behind her eyes. His mouth covered hers, taking her gasps and moans and, yes, even her cries of pleasure into him the way she still welcomed him into her body.

The bliss rippled through her in tingling aftershocks even as he rolled to his side, tucking her against his chest. He drew the covers over them and kissed the top of her head tenderly, stroking her back. His heart thumped hard and loud against her ear in time with her own racing pulse.

What the hell had just happened?

The best sex of her life.

And as the wash of desire cooled inside her that thought scared her more than a little. Already she wanted him again. Far too much. She needed distance to shore up her own defenses. Establishing her independence after her divorce had been damn difficult. She couldn't allow herself to turn clingy or needy again—no matter how amazing the orgasm.

Once his breathing evened out into a low snore, she eased herself from his arms, needing to think through what had just happened between them. She inched off the bed, slowly, carefully, her feet finally touching the carpet.

She tugged on her shirt and panties, the fabric gliding

across her well-loved body still oversensitized from the explosiveness of her release. She pulled open the door to the sitting area with more than a little regret.

"You're leaving?" His voice rumbled softly from the bed.

She turned toward him, keeping her head high. "Just returning to my room for the night."

Gauzy white curtains and his large lounging body gave off the air of a blond sheikh…. Good Lord, her mind was taking fanciful routes and fantasies.

"Uh-uh." He shook his head, sliding his hands behind his neck, broad chest all but calling to her to curl right back up again. "You're not ready to sleep together."

"I want to." God, did she ever want to.

"Glad to hear it. Hold on to that thought for our weekend together." He swung his feet to the floor and was beside her in a heartbeat. He kissed her just once, firmly but without moving, as if simply sealing his imprint on her.

As if she didn't already carry the feel of him in her every thought right now.

He stepped back into his room. "Sleep well, Alexa. We leave early for the island. Good night."

The door closing after him, he left her standing in the middle of the sitting room ready to burst into flames all over again.

From inside the chartered jet, Alexa felt the blazing sun flame its way up the morning sky on her way to a king's getaway. The Atlantic Ocean stretched out below, a small dot of an island waiting ahead.

Their destination.

Waking up late, she and Seth had been too rushed for

conversation. They'd dressed the kids and raced to the lobby just as the limousine arrived to pick them up along with Javier and his wife. The luxury ride to the small airport had given her the opportunity to double-check with Bethany and clear the schedule change. Bethany seemed so excited at the prospect of new contacts, she gave two thumbs-up. So there were no obstacles to Alexa's leaving. The ride had been so smooth and speedy she'd been whisked onto the jet before she'd even fully wiped the sleep from her eyes.

Breakfast had been waiting for them on the flight, although she'd been told they would land within a half hour. She had monitored the babies plucking up Cheerios, while nibbling on a *churro*—a Spanish doughnut. It had all seemed so normal, as if her insides weren't still churning from what had happened between her and Seth the night before.

And wondering what would happen when they landed on the isolated island for the weekend.

Her eyes gravitated to the open door leading to the cockpit where Seth flew the jet, Javier sitting in the copilot's seat. Their night together scrolled through her mind in lush, sensual detail. He'd touched her, aroused her, fulfilled her in ways she'd never experienced before. And while she was scared as hell of where this intense connection might lead her, she couldn't bring herself to walk away. Not yet.

Victoria touched her arm lightly. "They're both loners, but I think they're going to work well together."

"I'm sure they will." Loner? She hadn't thought of Seth quite that way, more brusque and businesslike. Except when he was around his kids, then he really opened up. Like he had when talking to her during their carriage ride.

And while making love, he'd held nothing back.

"Are you all right?" Victoria asked.

Alexa forced a smile. "Sorry to be so quiet." She searched for something to explain her preoccupation with a certain hot pilot only a few feet away. "It's just surreal that we would go to a king's home with babies in tow."

"Deposed king—and indulgent grandfather. If it makes you worry less, he's not in residence at the moment. He's visiting his doctors on the mainland, follow-ups on some surgery he had. We'll have the island all to ourselves, other than the staff and security, of course." She replenished the pile of Cheerios on Olivia's tray. The company that had stocked and cleaned the jet had done their job well. "The twins will find anything they need already there. He even keeps a sitter on staff."

"So none of the king's family is in residence at the moment? No other children?"

"None. The other family members have their own homes elsewhere. Since the family has reconciled, they're all visiting more often."

"More air travel." That explained why they were courting Jansen Jets.

"And more need for security with all these extra trips."

That also explained how Seth fit the bill all the better with his background in search and rescue, and security devices for airports. "How scary to have to worry so much about a regular family vacation."

Victoria huffed her blond bangs from her forehead.

"The press may have eased up from the initial frenzy, but they haven't backed off altogether. Even relatives have to be on guard—and stay silent at all times."

Alexa struggled not to squirm. She was used to the background checks that accompanied working at an airport. "I hear you. No speaking to the press."

"Their cousin Alys is still persona non grata after speaking to the press. She moved back to another family compound in South America. I guess you could say she's even in exile from the exiled."

"That's so sad, but understandable." Alexa had grown up in a privileged world, but these people took privileged to a whole new level.

When the silence stretched, she followed Victoria's puzzled stare and realized...Alexa closed her fist around her napkin. She'd been scrubbing a smudge on the silver tray obsessively. Her flatware was lined up precisely and she'd even brushed some powdered sugar into a tiny pile.

Smiling sheepishly, she forced her fists to unfurl and still. "When I'm nervous, I clean."

Victoria covered Alexa's hand with her own. "There's nothing to sweat, really."

Easier said than done when she'd barely survived her home life growing up. It was one thing to stand on the periphery of that privileged world, restoring order to the messes made by others. It was another thing entirely to step into the lushness of overindulgence that had once threatened to swallow her whole. But she was committed to this weekend. Literally. There was no escape.

She stared out the window at the island nestled in miles and miles of sparkling ocean. Palm trees spiked from the lush landscape. A dozen or so small outbuildings dotted a semicircle around a larger structure.

The white mansion faced the ocean in a U shape, constructed around a large courtyard with a pool. Details were spotty but she would get an up close view soon enough. Even from a distance she couldn't miss the grand scale of the sprawling estate, the unmistakable sort that housed royalty.

The plane banked as Seth lined up the craft with a thin islet alongside the larger island. A single strip of pristine concrete marked the private runway. As they neared, a ferry boat came into focus. To ride from the airport to the main island? They truly were serious about security.

She thought she'd left behind this kind of life when she'd cut ties with her parents. She'd been happy with her peripheral role, knowing what the rich needed but free of the complications of that life for herself.

Yet here she was.

Did she really want to even dip her toe in this sort of affluent world again? What choice did she have at the moment? Her gaze slid back to Seth. No choice really given how deeply she ached to be with him again.

Or maybe she had a choice after all: the option to take control on their next encounter rather than simply following his lead.

And she would make damn sure he was every bit as knocked of lance by the experience as she'd been.

The night unfolded for Seth, full of opportunities.

He'd concluded his deal with Javier and would spend tomorrow formulating plans for the future. He was ready to celebrate. With Alexa. Hopefully she would be in the same mindset.

He closed the door to the nursery where the twins would spend the night under the watchful eye of one of the resident nannies.

Just before their bedtime, he'd tried Pippa again, on the off chance she would pick up and could wish the kids good-night. She'd actually answered, sounding overly chipper, but cut the call short once he'd attempted to put Owen and Olivia on the line. Something about the whole conversation had been "off" but he couldn't put his finger on the exact problem.

Most likely because all he could think about right now was getting Alexa naked again.

He entered their quarters. More like a luxurious condominium within the mansion. He and Alexa had been given separate rooms in the second floor corner suite, but he hoped he could keep her distracted through the night until she fell asleep in his arms, exhausted by good sex.

Great sex.

Searching the peach and gray room, he didn't see signs of her other than her suitcase open on her bed. His shoes padded softly against the thick Persian rug past a sitting area with an eating space stocked more fully than most kitchens.

The quiet echoed around him, leaving him hyperaware of other sounds…a ticking grandfather clock in the hall…the crashing ocean outside… Through the double doors, the balcony was as large as some yards.

And Alexa leaned on the railing.

A breeze gusted from the ocean plastering her long

tiered sundress to her body, draping her curves in deep purple.

He stopped beside her. "Penny for them?"

She glanced at him sideways, the hem of her dress brushing his leg like phantom fingers. "No money for no work, remember? I've done nothing here to earn even a cent. The nanny takes over the kids, and I have to admit, she's good at charming them."

"You would rather they cried for you?"

"Of course not! I just…I like to feel useful. In control."

"Most women I know would be thrilled by an afternoon with a manicurist and masseuse."

"Don't get me wrong, I enjoy being pampered as much as anyone. In fact, I think you deserve a bit of relaxation yourself." She tapped a pager resting on the balcony wall. "The nanny can call if she needs us. What do you say we head down to the beach? I found the most wonderful cabana where we can talk."

Talk?

Not what he'd been fantasizing about for their evening together. But Alexa apparently had something on her mind, given the determined tilt of her chin. He took her hand in his. Her short nails were shiny with clear polish. The calluses on her fingers from cleaning had been softened and he felt the urge to make sure she never had to pick up a scrub brush ever again.

Keeping his hand linked with hers, he followed her down the winding cement steps toward the beach. She kicked off her sandals and waited for him to ditch his shoes and socks.

Hand in hand, they walked along the shore, feet sinking into the sand as they made their way toward a white cabana. With each step closer he could feel the tension ramping up in her body.

"I'd hoped today would offer you breaks, be a sort of vacation."

She glanced up, a smile flickering. "This is paradise. I've been in some impressive mansions over the years, but even I'm a floored by this place. No kidding royalty. Your business is going to a whole new level with this deal."

"That's the plan." So why did he still feel so... unsettled? He gestured inside the cabana where she'd ordered two low lounge chairs with a small table of refreshments between them.

Her eyes flickered wide for a second before she plunged inside, choosing a chair and eyeing the wine, cheese and grapes. She'd obviously planned this chance to...talk?

She wriggled her toes in the sand and plucked a grape. A wave curled up closer and she stretched her legs out until the water touched the tips of her feet. "This truly is paradise."

He dropped into the chair beside her. "Then why are you so tense?"

"Why do you want to know?"

"Why do you think?" He poured deep red wine into two crystal glasses and let his eyes speak as fully as his words.

She took one of the drinks by the stem and sipped. "Victoria called you a loner."

"Interesting." And he wasn't sure what that had to do with anything.

"You have so much family in Charleston, I hadn't thought of you that way." The wind rippled and flapped the three canvas walls of the cabana. "You do have family there, right? You called them when you found the babies, to ask for help."

"I have two cousins—Vic and Paige. I grew up with them in North Dakota when my parents died in a car accident." He reached for his wine. "Their SUV slid off the road in a storm when I was eleven." He downed half of the fine vintage as if it was water.

"I'm so sorry." She touched his wrist lightly as he replaced his drink.

"No need to feel sorry for me. I was lucky to have family willing to take me in." He hesitated. "My parents didn't have any assets when they died. My aunt and uncle never said anything about the extra mouth to feed, but I vowed I would pay them back."

"Look at you now. You've truly accomplished the amazing."

He stared out over the dark water and the darker night sky. "Too late to give anything to them… It took me a while to find my footing. Too long."

"Good God, Seth, you're all of what…"

"Thirty-eight."

"A self-made billionaire by thirty-eight." Her laugh stroked over his senses like the ocean breeze. "I wouldn't call that a slow start."

But he was still chasing dreams around the country. "I didn't set out on this path. I wanted to fly for the Air Force, even started ROTC at the University of Miami, but lost out on a medical snafu that isn't an issue anywhere but the Air Force. So I finished my degree and came home. Ran a flight school while flying my veterinarian cousin around to farms until the family all relocated to South Carolina."

He could feel her undivided attention on him. He wasn't sure why he was spilling all of this about himself, but somehow the words kept coming out. Strange as hell since she'd been on the mark in calling him a loner in spite of his large family.

"I wrestle with wanting to give my kids everything while worrying about teaching them working class values. I think about it a lot, how to help them have their own sense of accomplishment."

"The fact that you're even thinking about it says you're ahead of the game." She reached for his hand this time, linking her fingers and squeezing. "You do well by them."

He lifted her hand to kiss her wrist. "You grew up in a privileged world but came out with a strong work ethic. Any tips?"

She laughed bitterly. "My parents had shallow values, spending every penny they inherited to indulge themselves. My father bankrupted the family trust fund, or rather I should say they both did. Now, I have to work in order to eat like most of the rest of the world, which isn't a tragedy or sob story. Just a reality."

He'd known about her father's crappy management of the family's finances and sportswear line. But… "What about your marriage settlement?"

"We signed a prenup. My father's lawyers were worried Travis was a fortune hunter. I told Travis I didn't care about any contracts but he insisted." She spread her arms without letting go of his hands. "No alimony for either of us."

Frustration spiked inside him. "He doesn't care that you were left penniless? The jackass."

"Stop right there." She squeezed his hand insistently.

"I signed the prenup, too, and I don't want your sympathy."

"Okay, I hear you."

What was she thinking right now? He wished he was better at understanding the working of a woman's mind. He'd brought her to the island for seduction, and somehow, out here tonight, they'd ended up talking about things he didn't share with others. But Alexa had a way of kicking down barriers, and he'd had as much sharing as he could take for one night.

The rush of the ocean pulling at the sand under his feet seemed as if it tugged the rest of the world with it. He'd brought Alexa to this island for a reason: to seduce her so thoroughly he could work through this raw connection they felt.

Except, as he leaned in to kiss her, he was beginning to realize the chances of working her out of his system was going to be damn near impossible.

Her hand flattened to his chest. "Stop."

"What?" His voice came out a little strangled, but he held himself still. If a woman said no, that meant no.

"Last time we did this, you were the boss." She slid from her lounger and leaned over to straddle his hips. The warm core of her seared his legs even through her cotton dress and his slacks. "This time, Seth, I'm calling the shots."

Seven

Seth's brain went numb.

Did Alexa actually intend to have sex with him outside, in a seaside cabana? If so, she wouldn't get an argument from him. He was just surprised, since she'd insisted on leaving his bed the night before. He'd assumed she was more reserved given how she'd wanted to keep the light off.

Although the way she tugged at his shirttails, he couldn't mistake her intent, or her urgency.

Moonbeams bathed her in a dim amber glow. Still straddling his hips, Alexa yanked the hem free then ripped, popping the buttons, sending them flying into the sand. Surprise snapped through him just as tangibly. Apparently he'd underestimated her adventurous spirit.

Wind rolled in from the ocean across his bare chest. His body went on alert a second before her mouth flicked, licked and nipped at his nipple the way he'd lavished attention on her the night before.

He cupped her hips, his fingers digging into the cottony softness of her bunched dress. "I like the way you think, Alexa."

"Good, but you need to listen better." She clasped his wrists and pulled them away. "This is *my* turn to be in control."

"Yes, ma'am." Grinning at her, he rested his hands on the lounger's armrests, eager to see her next move.

Wriggling closer, she sketched her mouth over his, over to his ear. "You won't be sorry."

Her hands worked his belt buckle free, her cool fingers tucking inside to trace down the length of his arousal. He throbbed in response, wanted to ditch their clothes and roll her onto the sandy ground. The more she stroked and caressed, the more he ached to do the same to her. But every time he started to move, she stopped.

Once he stilled again, she nipped his ear or his shoulder, her fingers resuming the torturously perfect glide over him. His fingers gripped the rests tighter, until the blood left his hands.

Alexa swept his pants open further, shifting. As he started to move with her, she placed a finger over his lips. "Shh… I've got this."

Sliding from his lap, she knelt between his legs and took him in her mouth, slowly, fully. Moist, warm ecstasy clamped around him, caressed him. His head fell back against the chair, his eyes closing, shutting out all other sensation except the glide of her lips and tongue.

Her hands clamped on his thighs for balance. With

his every nerve tuned into the feel of her, even her fingers digging into his muscles ramped his pulse higher. Wind lifted her hair, gliding it over his wrist. The silky torment almost sent him over the edge.

The need to finish roared inside him, too much, too close. He wasn't going there without her. Time for control games to come to an end.

He clasped her under her arms and lifted her with ease, bringing her back to his lap.

"Condom," he growled through clenched teeth. "In my wallet. Leftover from the hotel."

Laughing softly, seductively, she reached behind him and tucked her fingers into his back pocket. The stroke of her hand over his ass had him gritting his teeth with restraint. Then she pitched his wallet to the ground with a wicked glint in her eyes.

What the hell?

She leaned sideways, toward the table of wine and cheese. Pitching aside a napkin, she uncovered a stack of condoms. "I came prepared."

His eyebrows rose at the pile of condoms, a dozen or so. "Ambitiously so."

"Is that a problem?" She studied him through her lashes.

God, he loved a challenge and this woman was turning out to be a surprise in more ways than one since she'd blasted into his life such a short time ago. "I look forward to living up to your expectations."

"Glad to hear it." She tore open one of the packets and sheathed him slowly.

Backlit by the crescent moon, she stood. She bunched the skirt of her dress and swept her panties down, kicking them aside. A low growl of approval rumbled inside him as he realized her intent. She straddled him again, inching the hem of her dress up enough so the hot heat of her settled against his hard-on.

Cradling his face in her hands, she raised up on her knees to kiss him. Her dress pooled around them, concealing her from view as she lowered herself onto the length of his erection. The moist clamp of her gripped him, drew him inside until words scattered like particles of sand along the beach.

The scent of the ocean clung to her skin. Unable to resist, he tasted her, trekking along her bared shoulder and finding the salty ocean flavor clung to her skin. He untied the halter neck of her dress, the fabric slithering down to reveal a lacy strapless bra. Her creamy breasts swelled just above the cups and with a quick flick of his fingers, he freed the front clasp.

Freed her.

Lust pumped through him along with anticipation. He filled his hands with the soft fullness, the shadowy beauty of her just barely visible in the moonlight.

His thumbs brushed the pebbly tips. "Someday we're going to make love on a beach with the sun shining down, or in a room with all the lamps on so I can see the bliss on your face."

"Someday..." she echoed softly.

Were those shadows in her eyes or just the play of clouds drifting past?

Her face lowered to his, blocking out the view and his thoughts as she sealed her mouth to his, demanding, giving and taking. With the lighting dim, his other senses heightened. The taste of her was every bit as intoxicating as the lingering hint of red wine on her tongue. Burying himself deep inside her, deeper still, he reveled in the purr of pleasure vibrating in her throat.

He stroked down her spine until his hands tucked under her bottom. Her soft curves in his palms, he angled her nearer, burning for more of her, more of them together. Her husky sighs and moans grew louder and closer together. Damn good thing since he was balancing on the edge himself, fulfillment right there for the taking.

Waves crashed in the distance, echoing the rush of his pulse pounding in his ears. Sand rode the air and clung to the perspiration dotting their skin, the gritty abrasion was arousing as she writhed against him. He tangled his hand into her satiny hair and gently tugged her head back. Exposing her breasts to his mouth, he took the tip of one tight bud and rolled it lightly between his teeth.

She sighed, her back arching hard and fast, her chanted "yes, yes, yes," circling him. Wrapping and pulsing around him like the moist spasms of her orgasm. Her cries of completion mingled with the roar of crashing waves.

Blasting through his own restraint.

Thrusting through her release, he triggered another in her just as he came. The force slammed through him, powerful and eclipsing everything else as he flew apart inside her into a pure flat spin nosedive into pleasure. His arms convulsed around her with the force of his completion.

He forced his fist open to release her hair even though she hadn't so much as whimpered in complaint. In fact, her head stayed back even as he relinquished her hair, the locks lifted and whipped by the wind into a tangled mass.

Gasping, she sagged on top of him, her bared breasts against his heaving chest. He didn't have a clue how long it took him to steady his breathing, but Alexa still rested in his arms. He retied the top of her sundress with hands not quite as steady as he would like. She nuzzled his neck with a soft, sated sigh.

He slid from under her, smoothing her dress over her hips, covering her with more than a little regret. With luck, though, there would be more opportunities to peel every stitch of clothing from her body.

For now, though, it was time to go inside. He refastened his pants and tucked the remaining condoms in his pocket. Not much he could do about his shirt since the buttons were scattered on the beach. He snagged the nursery pager and clipped it to his waistband before turning back to Alexa.

Scooping her in his arms, he started barefoot toward the mansion. She looped her arms around his neck, her head lolling onto his shoulder. Climbing the steps to their second floor suite, he walked through the patio filled with topiaries, ferns and flowering cacti. He'd enjoyed her power play on the beach. It had certainly paid off for both of them. But that didn't mean he was passing over control completely.

Tonight, she would sleep in his bed.

Alexa stretched in the massive sleigh bed, wrapped in the delicious decadence of Egyptian cotton sheets and the scent of making love with Seth. She stared around the unfamiliar surroundings, taking in oil paintings and heavy drapery.

She dimly remembered him carrying her from the beach to his bed. For a second, she'd considered insisting he take her to her room and leave her there. But his arms felt so good around her and she'd been so deliciously sated from their time in the cabana, she'd simply cuddled against his chest and slept.

God, had she ever slept. She couldn't remember when she'd last had eight uninterrupted hours. Could be because every muscle in her body had relaxed.

Yes, she knew she hadn't turned on the glaring lights, literally and in theory, by avoiding telling him about the issues in her past. But taking control last night had given her the confidence to invite Seth the rest of the way into her life.

Through the thick wood door, she heard voices in the other room; Seth's mingled with the babble of the twins. She smiled, looking forward to the day already. Except her suitcase and other clothes were in her bedroom, and she couldn't walk out there as is with the children nearby.

Swinging her feet to the floor, she grabbed her dress off the wing chair and pulled it on hastily. The crumpled cotton shouted that she'd spent the night with a man, but at least the twins wouldn't pick up on that. She could say "good morning" to them and then zip into her room to put on something fresh before she greeted the rest of the household.

At the door, she paused by a crystal vase of lisianthus with blooms that resembled blue roses. She plucked one out, snapped the stem and tucked the blossom behind her ear. Her hands gravitated to the flowers, straightening two of the blooms again so they were level with the rest, orderly. Perfect. She pulled open the door to the living area.

Another voice mingled in the mix.

An adult female voice.

Alexa froze in the open doorway. She scoured the room. Seth sat in a chair at the small writing desk, a twin on each knee as they faced the laptop computer in the middle of a Skype conversation.

A young woman's face filled the screen, her voice swelling from the speakers. "How are my babies? I've missed you both so very, very much."

Oh, God. It couldn't be. Not right now.

If Alexa had harbored any doubts as to the woman's identity, both babies chanted, "Ma-ma, Ma-ma, Ma-ma."

"Olivia, Owen, I'm here." Her voice echoed with obvious affection.

Pippa Jansen wasn't at all what she'd expected.

For starters, the woman didn't appear airheaded; in fact she had a simple, auburn-haired glamour. She wore a short-sleeved sweater set and pearls. From the log cabinlike walls and mountainous backdrop behind Pippa, she didn't appear to be at a plush spa or cruise ship getaway as Alexa had assumed.

Pippa didn't look to be partying or carefree. She appeared...tired and sad. "Mommy's just resting up, like taking a good nap, but I'll see you soon. We'll have yogurt and play in the sandbox. Kisses and hugs." She pressed a hand to her lips then wrapped her arms around herself. "Kisses and hugs."

Olivia and Owen blew exuberant baby kisses back. Both babies were so happy, so blissfully unaware. Alexa's heart ached for both of them. Her hands twitchy, she straightened a leather-bound volume of *Don Quixote* on a nearby end table.

Tension radiated from Seth's shoulders as he held a baby on each knee. "Pippa, while I understand your need for a break, I need some kind of reassurance that you're not going to drop off the map again once we hang up. I need to be able to reach you if there's an emergency."

"I promise." Her voice wavered. "I'll check in regularly from now on. I wouldn't have left this way if I wasn't desperate. I know I should have stayed to tell you myself, but I was scared you would say no, and I really needed a break. I watched through an airport window until you got on your plane. Please don't be angry with me."

"I'm not mad," he said, not quite managing to hide the irritation in his voice. "I just want to make sure you're all right. That you never feel desperate."

"This time away is good for me, really. I'll be back to normal when I come back to Charleston."

"You know I would like to have the children more often. When you're ready to come back, we can hire more help when they're with you, but we can't have a repeat of what happened at the airport. The twins' safety has to come first."

"You're right." She fidgeted with her pearls, her nails chewed down. "But I don't think we should talk about this now, in front of the babies."

"You're right, but we do have to discuss it. Soon."

"Absolutely." She nodded, almost frantically, pulling a last smile for the babies. "Bye-bye, be good for Daddy. Mommy loves you."

Her voice faded along with her picture as the

connection ended. Olivia squealed, patting the screen while Owen blew more kisses.

Alexa sagged against the door frame. She'd been prepared to hate Pippa for the way she'd been so reckless with her kids. And while she still wasn't ready to let the woman off the hook completely, she saw a mother running on fumes. Someone who was stressed and exhausted. She saw a mother who genuinely loved her children. Pippa had obviously reached her breaking point and had wisely taken them to their father before she snapped.

Of course sticking around to explain that to him would have been a far safer option. But life wasn't nearly as black and white as she'd once believed.

She'd seen Seth angry, frustrated, driven, affectionate, turned on… But right now, as Seth stared at the empty computer screen, she saw a broad-shouldered, good man who was deeply sad.

A man still holding conflicted feelings for his ex-wife.

Seth set each of his kids onto the floor and wished the weight on his shoulders was as easy to move.

Talking to Pippa had only made the situation more complicated just when he really could have used some simplicity in his personal life. He and Alexa had taken their relationship to a new level last night, both with the sex and sharing the bed. And he'd looked forward to cementing that relationship today—and tonight.

The call from Pippa had brought his life sharply back into focus. She was clearly at the end of her rope. While he wanted more time with his children, he didn't want to get it this way.

And this certainly wasn't how he'd envisioned kicking off his day with Alexa.

Glancing back over his shoulder at her in the doorway, he said, "You can come in now."

He'd sensed her there halfway through the conversation with his ex. Strange how he'd become so in tune with Alexa so quickly.

"I didn't mean to eavesdrop." She stepped deeper into the room, a barefoot goddess in her flowing purple dress with a flower behind her tousled hair.

Gracefully she sank down to the floor in front of the babies and a pile of blocks. He took in her effortless beauty, her ease with his kids. She was his dream woman—who'd come into his life at a nightmare time.

Right now, he couldn't help but be all the more aware of her strength, the way she met challenges head-on rather than running from her troubles. She'd rebuilt her entire life from the ground up. He admired that about her. Hell, he just flat out liked her, desired her and already dreaded the notion of watching her walk away.

"The conversation wasn't private." He shoved up from the chair and sat on the camelback sofa. "Olivia and Owen were just talking with their mother. Raising a baby is tough enough. The added pressure of twins just got to her. She's wise to take a break."

She glanced up sharply. "Even though she left them unattended on the airplane?"

"I'm aware that the way she chose to take that break left more than a little to be desired in the way of good judgment." He struggled to keep his voice level for the kids. For Alexa, too. He couldn't blame her for voicing the truth. "I'll handle it."

"Of course. It's really none of my business." She gnawed her bottom lip, stacking blocks then waiting for Olivia to knock the tower over. "Why don't I take the kids for a couple of hours? Give you some time to—"

"I've got them." He watched his son swipe his fist through the plastic blocks with a squeal of delight. "I'm sure you want a shower or a change of clothes."

In a perfect world he would have been joining her in that shower. As a matter of fact, in his screwed up, imperfect world he needed that shower with her all the more. What he would give for twenty minutes alone with her under the spray of hot water with his hands full of soap suds and naked Alexa. He swallowed hard and filed those thoughts away at the top of his "to do" list.

Although to get to everything on that list he would need more time. A lot more time.

"Really, it's no trouble." She patiently stacked the blocks again in alphabetical order while Olivia tried to wedge one, the *w*, in her mouth. "I'm getting good at balancing them on both hips. They can run out some energy on the beach while you finish up last minute busi—"

"I said I have them. They are my children," he snapped more curtly than he'd intended, but the discussion with Pippa had left him on edge. Wrestling for control was tough as hell with anger and frustration piling up inside him faster than those blocks made a Leaning Tower of Pisa.

Hurt slashed across her face before she schooled her features into an expressionless mask. "I'll change then, and take care of my own packing. How much longer until we leave the island?"

"We're flying out in an hour." Not that he intended to let that stop him from pursuing her. As much as he'd hoped to win her over during their trip, he now realized that wasn't going to be enough. He needed more—more time with her, more *of* her. While his relationship with Pippa had been a disaster, he was wiser for the experience now. He could enjoy Alexa in his life without letting himself get too entangled, too close.

Staring at his babies on the floor, he listened to the echo of tread as she walked away. Thought harder on the prospect of her walking away altogether.

Away, damn it.

He was going to lose Alexa if he didn't do something. He was fast realizing that no matter what his concerns about bringing a new woman into his children's lives, he couldn't let her leave.

"Alexa?"

Her footsteps stopped, but she didn't answer.

God, for about the hundredth time he wished they'd met a year from now when this would have been so much easier. But he couldn't change it. The time was now.

He wanted Alexa in his life.

"I'm sorry for being an—" He paused short of cursing in front of his children. "I'm sorry for being a jerk. I know you didn't sign on for this, but I hope you'll give me a chance to make it up to you."

She stayed silent so long he thought she would tell him to go to hell. He probably deserved as much for the way he was botching things with her right now. Her lengthy sigh reached him, heaping an extra dose of guilt on his shoulders.

"We'll talk later, after you have your children settled."

"Thanks, that's for the best." Problem was, with Pippa, he wasn't sure how or when things in his life would ever be *settled*. All the more reason to keep his emotions in check when dealing with either woman in his life. Starting now.

Because, their island paradise escape was over. It was time to return to the real world.

Riding on the ferry out to the king's private airstrip, Alexa gripped the railing as they neared Seth's plane on the islet runway. The twins, buckled into their safety seats, squealed in delight at the sea air in their faces as they waved goodbye to the tropical paradise.

She feared she was saying goodbye to far more than that.

Her eyes trekked to Seth, who was standing with the boat captain. Not surprising, since Seth had all but shut down emotionally around her since his conversation with his ex-wife.

Alexa twirled the stem of a sea oat in her hand, then tickled the twins' chins with it. They were cute, but it would be helpful if they spoke a few more words so they could hold up the other end of a conversation. There was no one else to talk to. Javier and his wife had opted to stay on the island for a couple of extra days. Alexa envied them. Deeply. The time here with Seth before that Skype call had been magical, and she wanted more.

As smoothly as the ferry moved along the marshy water, her mind traveled to dreams of extending her relationship with Seth. Could what they'd shared be just as powerful under the pressure of everyday life?

A daunting thought to say the least, especially when he had begun pulling away after his conversation with Pippa.

Thinking of that call, Alexa reached for her own phone. She should check for messages from Bethany. She'd turned her cell off last night and let it recharge— and, yes, probably because she didn't want interruptions. The way she'd made love with Seth on the beach...the way he'd made love to her afterward...

Heat pooled inside her, flushing her skin until she could have sworn she had an all-over sunburn.

Her phone powered up and she checked... No messages from Bethany, but the expected nine missed calls from her mother. Just as she started to thumb them away, the phone rang in her hand.

Her mom.

She winced.

Was her mother's perfectly coiffed blond hair actually a satellite dish that detected when her daughter turned on her phone?

Wind tearing at her own loose hair, she considered ignoring that call altogether as she had the others. But Olivia giggled and Alexa's heart tugged. If she felt this much for these two little ones so quickly, how much more must her mother feel for her?

Guilt nudged her to answer. "Hey, Mom. What's up?"

"Where are you, Lexi? I have been calling and calling." Laughter and the clank of dishes echoed over the phone line. Her parents had taken what little cash they had left and bought into a small retirement community chock-full of activities. How they continued to pay the bills was a mystery. "Lexi? Are you listening?

I took a break from my 'Mimosas and Mahjong' group just to call you."

God, why couldn't her mother call her Alexa instead of Lexi? "Working. In Florida."

Crap. Why hadn't she lied?

And was the island even part of Florida? Or was it the royal family's own privately owned little kingdom? She wasn't sure and didn't intend to split hairs—or reveal anything more than necessary to her mother.

"Oh, are you near Boca? Clear the rest of your day," her mother ordered. "Your dad and I will drive over to meet you."

"I really am working. I can't just put that on hold. And besides, I'm in Northern Florida. Very far away." Not far enough at the moment.

"You can't be working. I hear children in the background."

She hated outright lying. So she dodged with, "The boss has kids."

"Single boss?"

Not wading into those waters with her mother. "Why was it that you called?"

"Christmas!"

Huh? "The holidays are months away, Mom."

"I know, but we need to get these things pinned down so nothing goes wrong. You know how I like to have everything perfect for the holidays."

And that need for perfection differed from the rest of the year how, exactly? "I'll do my best to be there."

"I need to know, though, so we have an even number of males and females at the table. I would just hate to have the place setting ruined at the last minute if you cancel."

So much for her mother's burning need to see her only child. She just needed an extra warm body at the table, a body with female chromosomes. "You know what, Mom, then let's just plan on me not being there."

"Now, Lexi, don't be that way. And wipe that frown off your face. You're going to get wrinkles in your forehead early, and I can't afford collagen treatments for you."

Deep breaths. She wasn't her mother. She'd refused to let her mom have power over her life.

But control seemed harder to find today than usual after she'd lowered so many barriers with Seth last night.

Her mother had her own reasons for the way she acted, most of which came from having a control freak mother of her own. Holiday photos were always color-coordinated, perfectly posed and very strained.

But understanding the reasons didn't mean accepting the hurtful behavior. Alexa had worked hard to break the cycle, to get well and make sure that if she ever had a child of her own, the next generation would know unconditional love, rather than the smothering oppression of a parent determined to create a perfectly crafted mini-me.

Her eyes slid down to Olivia who was trying her best to stuff her sock in her mouth. God, that kid was adorable.

Alexa's hand tightened around the phone, another swell of sympathy for her mom washing over her. She could do this. She could talk to her mother while still keeping boundaries in place. "Mom, I appreciate that you want to have me there for the holidays. I will get back to you at the end of the month with a definite answer one way or the other."

"That's my good girl." Her mother paused for a second, the background chatter and cheers the only indication she was still on the line. "I love you, Alexa. Thanks for picking up."

"Sure, Mom. I love you, too."

And she did. That's what made it so tough sometimes. Because while love could be beautiful, it also stole control, giving another person the power to cause hurt.

As the ferry docked at the airstrip and Alexa dropped the phone back into her bag, her eyes didn't land on the kids this time. Her gaze went straight to Seth.

Eight

Her stomach knotted with each step down the stairway leading from the private jet. Back where she'd started in Charleston a few short, eventful days ago.

The flight hadn't given them any opportunity to discuss what they would do after landing. The kids had been fussy for most of the journey, not surprising given all the upheaval to their routine. Seth had been occupied with flying the plane through bumpy skies.

And all those pockets of turbulence hadn't helped the children's moods. Or hers for that matter. Her nerves were shot.

Alexa hitched Olivia on her hip more securely. The early morning sun glinted off the concrete parking area of the private airport that housed Jansen Jets. She saw Seth's world with new eyes now. Before she'd viewed him and his planes from a business perspective. She'd seen his hangars at the private airport and his jets, and thought about what a boon it would be to service his fleet. Now, she took in the variety of aircraft, in awe of how much he'd acquired in such a short time.

From her research on him she'd learned that about ten years ago he'd purchased the privately owned airport, which, at that time, sported two hangars. Now there were three times as many filled with anything from the standard luxury Learjets to Gulfstreams like the one she'd flown in today. In fact, one of those Lears taxied out toward the runway now.

As she looked back at the hangars, she also saw smaller Cessnas. Perhaps for flight training like he'd done back in North Dakota? Or was that a part of the search and rescue aspect he obviously felt so passionately about?

There was so much more to Seth than she'd originally thought.

An open hangar also gave her a peek of what appeared to be a vintage plane, maybe World War II era. Not exactly what she expected a buttoned-up businessman to own. But a bold, crop-dusting North Dakota farm boy who'd branched out to South Carolina, who'd built a billion-dollar corporation from the ground up? That man, she could envision taking to the skies in the historic craft.

She'd wanted to get to know more about Seth, to understand him, at first to win his contract and then to protect herself from heartache. Instead she was only more confused, more vulnerable, and unable to walk away.

Her feet hit solid ground just as she heard a squeal from the direction of the airport's main building, a one-story red brick structure with picture windows. An auburn-haired woman raced past a fuel truck toward the plane, her arms wide.

Pippa Jansen.

The beauty wore the same short-sleeve sweater set she'd had on during the Skype conversation earlier. She raced toward them, a wide smile on her face.

Olivia stretched out her hands, squealing, "Ma-ma, Ma-ma..."

Pippa gathered her daughter into her arms and spun around. "I missed you, precious girl. Did you have fun with Daddy? I have your favorite *Winnie the Pooh* video in the car."

She slowed her spin, coming face-to-face with Alexa. A flicker of curiosity chased through Pippa's hazel eyes. The Learjet engines hummed louder in the background as the plane accelerated, faster, faster, swooping smoothly upward. Owen pointed with a grin as he clapped.

Her son's glee distracted her and she turned to kiss his forehead. "Hello, my handsome boy."

His face tight with tension, Seth passed over his son. "I thought we were going to talk later today?"

"I decided to meet you here instead. After I heard the children's voices this morning, I just couldn't stay away any longer. I missed them too much, so I flew straight home. Your secretary gave me your arrival time since it related to the children." She kissed each child on top of the head, breathing deeply before looking up again, directly at Alexa. "And who might you be?"

Seth stepped up, his face guarded. "This is my friend Alexa. She took time off work to help me with the twins since I had an out of town business meeting I couldn't cancel. Your note said you were going to be gone for two weeks."

"The weekend's rest recharged me. I'm ready to be with my children again." Her pointy chin jutted with undeniable strength. "It's my custodial time."

He sighed wearily, guiding them toward the building, away from the bustle of trucks and maintenance personnel. He stopped outside a glass door at the end of the brick building. "Pippa, I don't want a fight. I just want to be sure you won't check out on them again without notice."

"My mother's in the car. I'm staying with her for a while." She adjusted the weight of both babies, resettling them. "Seth, I'm going to take you up on the offer to hire extra help when I'm with them, and I'd like to write up more visitation time into our agreement. They've been weaned for a couple of months, so the timing is right. Okay?"

He didn't look a hundred percent pleased with the outcome but nodded curtly. "All right, we'll meet tomorrow morning in my office at ten to set that in motion."

"Good, I'm so relieved to see them. My time away gave me a fresh perspective on how to pace myself better." She passed Olivia to Seth. "Could you help me carry them out to the car? You'll get to see my mom and reassure yourself." She glanced at Alexa. "You won't mind if I borrow him for a minute?"

"Of course not." It was clear Alexa wasn't invited on this little family walk.

Seth slid an arm around Alexa's shoulder. "This won't take long." He pulled out a set of keys and unlocked the glass door in front of him. "You can wait in my office space here where it's cooler."

An office here? Jansen Jets Corporate was located downtown. But then of course he would have an office here as well.

"I'll be waiting."

He dropped a kiss on her lips. Nothing lengthy or overtly sexual, but a clear branding of their relationship in front of his ex. Surprise tingled through her along with the now expected attraction.

Pippa looked at her with deepening curiosity. "Thank you for being there for my babies when Seth needed an extra set of hands."

Alexa didn't have a clue how to respond, so she opted for a noncommittal. "Owen and Olivia are precious. I'm glad I could help."

Stepping into the back entrance to Seth's office, she crossed to a corner window and watched the couple carrying their children toward a silver Mercedes sedan parked and idling. Pippa's older "twin" sat behind the wheel. Her mother, no doubt.

A sense of déjà vu swept over Alexa at the mother-daughter twin look. It could have been her with her own mom years ago. More than the outward similarity, Alexa recognized a fragility in Pippa, something she'd once felt herself, a lack of ego. Having rich parents provided a lot of luxuries, but it could also rob a person of any sense of accomplishment. Her parents bought her everything, even bought her way out of bad grades... which had been wrong.

Just as it would be wrong to write off Pippa's reckless escape from motherhood for the weekend. Yes, she was an overwhelmed mom, but she was also a parent with resources. She could hire help. There were a hundred better options than leaving her children unattended on an aircraft. Pippa's excuse about watching through a window was bogus. How could she have helped them from so far away if something had gone wrong?

Alexa's fists dug into the windowsill, helplessness sweeping over her. There was nothing she could do. These weren't her children. This wasn't her family. She had to trust Seth to handle the situation with his ex-wife.

Spinning back to the office, she studied the space Seth had created for himself. It was a mass of contradictions, just like the man himself. High-end leather furniture filled the room, a sofa, a wing recliner and office chair, along with thick mahogany shelves and a desk.

She also saw a ratty fishing hat resting on top of a stack of books. The messy desktop was filled with folders and even a couple of honest to God plastic photo cubes—not exactly what she'd expected in a billionaire's space. It was tough for her to resist the desire to order the spill of files across the credenza.

Forcing her eyes upward, she studied the walls packed with framed charts and maps, weathered paper with routes inked on them. In the middle of the wall, he'd displayed a print of buffalo on the plains tagged Land of Tatanka.

The land looked austere and lonely to her. Like the man, a man who'd been strangely aloof all day. Her fingers traced along the bottom of the frame. Even as he embraced the skies and adventure here, there was still a part of him that remembered his stark North Dakota farm boy roots.

The opening door pulled her attention off the artwork

and back to the man striding into the room. His face was hard. His arms empty and loose by his sides.

She rested her hand on his shoulder and squeezed lightly. "Are you okay?"

"I will be." He nodded curtly, stepping away.

Only a few minutes earlier he'd kissed her and now he was distant, cold. Had it been an act? She didn't think so. But if he didn't want her here, if he needed space, she could find her own way home. She started toward the door leading out of his office and into the building.

"Alexa," he called out. "Hold on. We have some unfinished business."

Business? Not what she was hoping to hear. "What would that be?"

He walked to the massive desk and pulled a file off the corner. "I made a promise when you agreed to help me. Before I spoke to Pippa this morning, I put in some calls, arranged for you and your partner to interview with four potential clients who commute into the Charleston area, both at the regional airport and here at my private airstrip." He passed her the folder. "Top of the list, Senator Matthew Landis."

She took the file from his hand, everything she could have hoped for when she'd first stepped onto his plane, cleaning bucket in hand. And now? She couldn't shake the sense he was shuffling her off, giving her walking papers. While, yes, that's what they'd agreed upon, she couldn't help worrying that he was fulfilling the deal to the letter so they could be done, here and now.

Her grip tightened on the file until the edges bent. "Thank you, that's great. I appreciate it."

"You still have to seal the deal when you meet them, but I had my assistant compile some notes I made that I believe will help you beef up your proposal." He sat on the edge of the desk, picked up a photo cube and tossed it from hand to hand. "I also included some ways I think you may be missing out on expansion opportunities."

He hadn't left money on the dresser, by God, but somehow the transaction still felt cheap given the bigger prize they could have had together.

"I don't know how to thank you." She clasped the folder to her chest and wondered why this victory felt hollow. Just a few days ago she would have turned cartwheels over the information in that folder.

"No. Thank *you*. It was our agreement from the start, and I keep my word." *Toss, toss,* the cube sailed from hand to hand. "And while I am genuinely sorry I can't pass over my fleet to A-1, I have requested that your company be called first for any subcontracting work from this point on."

His words carried such finality she didn't know whether to be hurt or mad. "That's it then. Our business is concluded."

"That was my intention." He pitched the cube side to side, images of Owen and Olivia tumbling to rest against a paperweight.

Okay, she was mad, damn it. They'd slept together. He'd kissed her in plain view of his ex-wife. She deserved better than this.

She slapped the file down on his messy desk and yanked the cube from midair. "Is this a brush-off?"

He did a double take and took his photos back from her. "What the hell makes you think that?"

"Your ice cold shoulder all day, for starters." She crossed her arms over her chest.

"I'm clearing away business because from this point

on, if we see each other, it's for personal reasons only." He clasped her shoulders, skimming his touch down until she stepped into his embrace. "No more agendas. Holding nothing back."

She looked up at him. "Then you're saying you want to spend more time together?"

"Yes, that's exactly what I'm telling you. You've cleared your calendar until tomorrow, and it's not even lunchtime yet. So let's spend the day together, no kids, no agendas, no bargains." He brushed her hair back with a bold, broad palm. "I can't claim to know where this is headed, and there are a thousand reasons why this is the wrong time. But I can't just let you walk away without trying."

Being with this guy was like riding an emotional yo-yo. One minute he was intense, then moody, then happy, then sensual. And she was totally intrigued by all of him. "Okay then. Ask me out to lunch."

A sigh of relief shuddered through him, his arms twitching tighter around her waist. "Where would you like to go? Anywhere in the country for lunch. Hell, we could even go out of the States for supper if you can lay hands on your passport."

"Let's keep it stateside this time." This time? She shivered with possibility. "As for the place? You pick. You're the one with the airplanes."

With those words, reality settled over her with anticipation and more than a little apprehension. She'd committed. This wasn't about the babies or her business any longer. This was about the two of them.

She'd explored the complex layers of this man, and now she needed to be completely open to him as well.

They had one last night away from the real world to decide where to go next.

One last night for her to see how he handled knowing everything about her, even the insecure, vulnerable parts that were too much like those she'd seen in his ex-wife.

Seth parked the rental car outside the restaurant, waiting for Alexa's verdict on the place he'd chosen.

He could have taken her to Le Cirque in New York City or City Zen in D.C. He could have even gone the distance for Savoy's in Vegas. But thinking back over the things she'd shared about her past, he realized she wasn't impressed with glitz or pretension. They'd just left a king's island, for Pete's sake. Besides, she'd grown up with luxurious trappings and, if anything, seemed to disdain them now.

The North Dakota farm boy inside him applauded her.

So he'd fueled up one Cessna 185 floatplane and taken off for his favorite "hole-in-the-wall" eating establishment on the Outer Banks in North Carolina. A seaside clapboard bar, with great beer, burgers and fresh catch from the Atlantic.

A full-out smile spread across her face. "Perfect. The openness, the view... I love it."

Some of the cold weight he'd been carrying in his chest since saying goodbye to his kids eased. He sprinted around the front of the 1975 Chevy Caprice convertible—special ordered, thanks to his assistant's speedy persistence. He opened the door for Alexa. She swept out, her striped sundress swirling around her knees as she climbed the plank steps up to the patio dining area. The Seat Yourself sign hammered to a wooden column was weatherworn but legible.

He guided her to a table for two closest to the rocky shoreline as a waitress strolled over.

"Good to see you, Mr. Jansen. I'll get your Buffalo blue-water tuna bites and two house brews."

"Great, thanks, Carol Ann." Seth passed the napkin-rolled silverware across the table. Alexa fidgeted with the salt and pepper shakers until he asked, "Something wrong? Would you like to go somewhere else after all?"

She looked up quickly. "The place is great. Really. It's just... Well... I like to order my own food."

"Of course. I apologize. You're right, that was presumptuous of me." He leaned back in his chair. "Let me get Carol Ann back over and we can add whatever you would like."

"No need. Truly. It's just for future reference. And I actually do like the sound of what you chose, so it's probably silly that I said anything at all." She smiled sheepishly. "You may have noticed I have some... control issues."

"You appreciate order in your world. Plenty to admire about that." God knows, his world could stand a little more order and reason these days. The unresolved mess with Pippa still knocked around in his head. "That's a great asset in your job—"

He stopped short as the waitress brought their plates of Buffalo tuna bites, mugs of beer and glasses of water.

Alexa tore the paper off her straw and stirred her lemon wedge in her water. "Control's my way of kicking back at my childhood."

"In what way?" He passed an appetizer plate to her.

"When I was growing up there wasn't a lot I could

control without bringing down the wrath of Mom." She speared the fish onto her plate. "She may have depended on those nannies to free up her spa days and time on the slopes but her expectations were clear."

"And those were?"

"Great grades, of course, with all the right leadership positions to get into an Ivy League school. And in my 'spare time' she expected a popular, pretty daughter. Perfectly groomed, with the perfect boyfriend." She stabbed a bite and brought it to her mouth. "Standard stuff."

"Doesn't sound standard or funny to me." Out of nowhere, an image flashed through his mind of Pippa sitting in the front seat of the car with her mother, both women wearing matching sweater sets and pearls with their trim khakis.

"You're right. That kind of hypercontrol almost inevitably leads to some kind of rebellion in teens. Passive aggressive was my style in those days. The problem started off small and got worse. I controlled what I ate, when I ate, how much I ate." She chewed slowly.

A chill shot through him as he recalled her ordering the blocks for his kids. Her careful lining up of her silverware. Little things he'd written off as sweet peculiarities of a woman who liked the proverbial ducks in a row.

Now, his mind started down a dark path and he hoped to God she would take them on a detour soon. He didn't know what to say or do, so he simply covered her other hand with his and stayed quiet.

"Then I learned I could make Mom happy by joining the swim team. And what do you know? That gave me another outlet for burning calories. I felt good, a real rush of success." She tossed aside her fork. "Until one day when I peeled away my warm-up suit and I saw the looks of horror on the faces of the people around me..."

Squeezing her hand softly, he wished like hell he could have done something for her then. Wishing he could do something more now than just listen.

"I'm lucky to be alive actually. That day at swim practice, right after I saw the looks on their faces, I tried to race back to the locker room, but my body gave out... I pretty much just crumpled to the ground." She looked down at her hands fidgeting with the silverware. "My heart stopped."

He clasped her hand across the table, needing to feel the steady, strong beat of her heart throbbing in her wrist. There were no words he could offer up right now. But then he'd always been better at listening than talking anyway.

"Thank goodness the coach was good at CPR," she half joked, but her laugh quickly lost its fizz. "That's when my parents—and I—had to face up to the fact that I had a serious eating disorder."

She pulled away from him and rubbed her bare arms in spite of the noonday sun beating overhead. "I spent my senior year in a special high school—aka hospital— for recovering bulimics and anorexics." She brushed her windswept hair back with a shaky hand. "I was the latter, by the way. I weighed eighty-nine pounds when they admitted me."

This was more—worse—than he'd expected and what he'd expected had been gut-twisting enough. He thought of his own children, of Olivia, and he wanted to wrap her up in cotton while he read every parenting book out there in hopes that he could spare his kids this kind of pain. "I'm so damn sorry you had to go through that."

"Me, too. I'm healthy now, completely over it, other than some stretch marks from the seesawing weight loss and gain."

"Was that why you preferred to keep the lights off?"

"When we were making love? Yes." She nodded, rolling her eyes. "It's not so much vanity as I wasn't ready to tell you this. I fully realize those lines on my skin are a small price to pay to be alive." She reached for her beer, tasted the brew once, and again, before placing the mug on the red-checkered cloth. "My stint in the special high school cost me a real prom, sleepovers with ice cream sundaes and dates spent parking with a boyfriend. But it also screwed up Mom's Ivy League aspirations for me. So I won control of something for a while, I guess."

"What happened after you graduated?"

"Dad bought my way into a college, and I married the man of their choice." She patted her chest. "A-1 Cleaning is the first independent thing I've done on my own, for me."

Admiration for her grew, and he'd already been feeling a hefty dose where she was concerned. But she'd broken away from every support system she had in place—such as they were—to forge her own path. Turning her back on her family had to be tough, no matter how strained the relationship. He could also see she'd grown away from the world Pippa still seemed to be suffocating in.

He hadn't been expecting this kind of revelation from her today. But he knew he'd better come up with the right response, to offer the affirmation she should have gotten from those closest to her.

"What other things would you like to do? Anything… I will make it happen."

She leaned back in her chair, her eyes going whimsical. "That's a nice thought. But the things I regret? I need to accept I can't have them and be at peace with that."

"Things such as?"

"I can't go back and change my teenage years. I need to accept that and move forward."

The sadness in her voice as she talked about her lost past sucker punched him with the need to do something for her. To give her back those parts of her life her parents had stolen by trying to live out their own dreams through their kid. He couldn't change the past.

But he could give her one of those high school experiences she'd been denied.

Nine

Alexa shook her hair free as they drove along the seaside road with the convertible top down. She adored his unexpected choices, from the car to the restaurant. The red 1975 Chevy Caprice ate up the miles down the deserted shore of the Outer Banks. She'd marveled at how lucky they were to get such a classic car, but then learned Seth's assistant had taken care of the arrangements.

How easy it was to forget he was a billionaire sometimes, with all the power and perks that came with such affluence.

The afternoon sun blazed overhead, glinting on the rippling tide. Sea oats and driftwood dotted the sandy beach along with bare picket fences permanently leaning from the force of the wind. Kind of like her.

Leaning and weathered by life, but not broken, still standing.

She studied the brooding man beside her. Seth drove on, quietly focused on the two-lane road winding ahead of them. What had he thought of her revelations at lunch? He'd said all the right things, but she could see his brain was churning her words around, sifting through them. She couldn't help but feel skittish over how he would treat her now. Would he back away? Or worse yet, act differently?

Tough to tell when he'd been in such an unpredictable mood since talking with Pippa. That made Alexa wonder if she should have waited to dish out her own baggage? But she couldn't escape the sense of urgency pushing her, insisting they had only a narrow slice of time. That once they returned to Charleston permanently, this opportunity to fully know him would disappear.

She hooked her elbow on the open window, her own face staring back at her in the side mirror. "Seth? Where are we going? I thought the airport was the other way."

"It is. I wanted to make the most of the day before we leave." He pointed ahead toward a red brick lighthouse in the distance. "We're headed there, on that bluff."

The ancient beacon towered in the distance. She could envision taking the kids there for a picnic, like the one they'd shared at the fort in St. Augustine. "It's gorgeous here. I love our South Carolinian low country home, but this is special, too, different. I can't believe I've never been here before."

Her parents had always opted for more "exotic" vacations.

"I thought you would appreciate it. You seem to have

an eye for the unique, an appreciation for entertainment off the beaten path."

"I'm not sure I follow what you mean."

"Like when we had the picnic at the old fort. You saw it with an artist's eye rather than looking for an up-to-date, pristine park. Must be the art history major in you. This place and this car are certainly pieces of history. Did I read you right on that?"

"You did, very much so." The fact that he knew her this well already, had put so much thought into what she thought, made her heart swell. The twisting road led higher over the town, taking them farther away and into a more isolated area.

When she looked around her, she also realized... "You brought me here to make out, didn't you?"

"Guilty as charged."

"Because of what I said at the restaurant about missing the high school experience of parking and making out with a guy."

"Guilty again. It's private, bare, stripped away nature, which in some ways reminds me of North Dakota as a whole. There's something...freeing about leaving civilization behind." He steered the car off the paved road, onto a dirt trail leading toward the lighthouse. "It's good to leave baggage behind, and it's safe to say we both have our fair share."

Nerves took flight in her belly like the herons along the shore. "Like what I told you at lunch?"

"In part. Yes." Tires crunched along the rocky road, spitting a gritty cloud of dirt behind them. "It's clear we're both members of the Walking Wounded Divorce Club, both with hang-ups. But we have something else in common, an attraction and a mutual respect."

The way he'd analyzed them chilled her in spite of the bold shining sun overhead and the thoughtfulness of his gesture. He'd pinpointed them so well, and yet… "You make it sound so logical. So calculated. So… coldly emotionless."

Stopping the car at the base of the lighthouse, the top of the bluff, he gripped the steering wheel in white-knuckled fists. "Believe me, there's nothing cold about the way I'm feeling about you. I want you so much I'm damn near ready to explode just sitting beside you."

Breathless, she leaned against her door, the power of his voice washing over her as tangibly as the sun warming her skin.

He turned toward her, leather seat squeaking, his green eyes flinty. "Just watching you walk across the room, I imagine resting my hands on your hips to gauge the sway." His fingers glided along her shoulder. "Or when I see the wind lift your hair, I burn to test the texture between my fingers. Everything about you mesmerizes me."

Tension crackled between them like static in her hair, in his words. "Before this past weekend, I'd been celibate for over six months. Attractive women have walked into my life and not one of them has tempted me the way you do."

There was no missing the intensity of his words—or the intent in his eyes. His fingers stroked through her hair, down to the capped sleeves of her sundress, hovering, waiting. "Did anyone ever tell you what a truly stunning woman you are, how beautiful you will still be when you're eighty-five years old? Not that it matters what the hell I, or anyone else, thinks."

While she was flattered, his words also left her blushing with self-consciousness.

She resisted the urge to fidget. "Okay, I hear you. Now could you stop? I don't need you to flatter me because of what I said earlier. I'm beyond needing affirmation of my looks."

"I'm not flattering. I'm stating facts, indisputable, beyond perceptions."

She realized now that he'd brought her out to this place for a private conversation, a better place to discuss her past than a crowded restaurant. She should have realized that earlier.

"Thank you and I hear you. Skewed perceptions played a part in what I went through." Her hands fell to his chest. "But I'm over that now. It was hard as hell, but I'm healthy and very protective of that particular fact."

"Good. I'm glad to hear it, and I don't claim to be an expert on the subject. I only know that I want to tell you how beautiful, how sexy you are to me. Yet, that seems to make you uncomfortable."

The ocean breeze lifted her hair like a lover's caress, the scent so clean and fresh that the day felt like a new beginning.

"Maybe I like to speak with actions."

"I'm all about that, too." His hands brushed down the sleeves of her dress. "When I touch you, it turns me inside out to feel the curves, the silky softness, the way you're one hundred percent a woman."

He inched the bodice down farther, baring the top of her breasts.

Realization raised goose bumps along her skin as she

grasped his deeper intent for bringing her here... "Are you actually planning for us to make love, here?"

He nuzzled the crook of her neck. "Do you think you're the only one who can initiate outdoor sex?"

"That was at night."

"Hidden away where no one could see us." Where they could barely see each other.

Her thoughts cleared as if someone had turned the sun up a notch. Out here, there was no turning off the lamp or shrouding herself in darkness. Oh hell, maybe she wasn't as over the past as she'd thought. She'd controlled everything about their lovemaking before.

This place, now, out in the brightest light of all, meant giving over complete control. That sent jitters clear through her. But the thought of saying no, of turning down this chance to be with him, upset her far more.

He cupped her face in both hands. "Do you think I would ever place you at risk? I chose this place carefully because I feel certain we're completely alone."

Alone and yet so totally exposed by the unfiltered sunshine. Seth was asking for a bigger commitment from her. He was requiring her trust.

Toying with his belt, she said, "Out here, huh? In full daylight. No drawing the shades, that's for sure."

"Sunscreen?" He grinned.

She raised an eyebrow and tugged his belt open. "You expect to be naked that long? You're a big talker."

His smile faded, his touch got firmer. "So you're good with this."

"I'm good with *you*," she murmured against his lips.

"I like the sound of that." He slanted his mouth over hers.

The man knew how to kiss a woman and kiss her well. The way he devoted his all to the moment, to her, in his big bold way, made her want to take everything he offered here today. She'd shared everything about herself at lunch. Giving all here seemed the natural extension of that if she dared.

And she did.

Easing back from him, she shrugged the sleeves of her dress down, revealing herself inch by inch, much the way he'd undressed for her their first time together. In some ways, this was a first for them. A first without barriers.

Her bodice pooled around her waist. With the flick of her fingers, she opened the front clasp on her lacy bra. And waited. It was one thing to bare herself in the dark, but in the daylight, everything showed, her journey showed. Her battle with anorexia had left stretch marks. Regaining her muscle tone had taken nearly six years.

Meeting his gaze, she saw…heat…passion…and tenderness. He touched her, his large hands so deft and nimble as they played over her breasts in just the ways she enjoyed best, lingering on *her* erogenous zones, the ones he must have picked up on from their time together.

She arched into his palms, her grip clenching around his belt buckle. Her head fell to rest against the leather seat. The sun above warmed every inch of her bared flesh as fully as his caresses, his kisses.

His hands swept down to inch the hem upward until he exposed her yellow lace panties. Just above the waistband, he flicked a finger against her belly button ring.

She smiled at a memory. "That was my treat to myself the first time I wore a bikini in public."

"I'll buy you dozens, each one with a different jewel."

Laughing softly, she traced his top lip with the tip of her tongue. He growled deeply in his throat. But he only allowed her to steal control for an instant before he stroked lower, dipping a finger inside her panties, between her legs, finding her wet and ready.

Her spine went weak and he braced her with an arm around her waist, holding her. She unbuttoned his shirt, sweeping it aside and baring his brazened chest to her eyes, her touch. The rasp of his crisp blond hair tantalized her fingertips.

She inhaled the scent of leather and sea, a brand-new aphrodisiac for her. "We should move this to the backseat where we can stretch out somewhat."

"Or we can stay here and save the backseat for later."

She purred her agreement as she swung her leg over to straddle his lap. The steering wheel at her back only served to keep her closer to him. Everything about this place was removed from the real world, and she intended to make the most of it. She opened his pants and somehow a condom appeared in his hand. She didn't care where or how. She just thanked goodness he had the foresight.

His hands palmed her waist, her arms looping around his neck. He lowered her onto him, carefully, slowly filling her. Moving within her. Or was she moving over him? Either way, the sensation rippled inside her, built to a fever pitch. Every sensation heightened: the give of the butter-soft leather under her knees, the rub of his trousers against the inside of her thighs.

The openness of the convertible and the untouched

landscape called to her. The endless stretch of ocean pulled at her, like taking a skein of yarn and unraveling it infinitely. Moans swelled inside her, begging to be set free to fly into that vastness.

He thrust his hands into her hair and encouraged her in a litany detailing how damn much he wanted her, needed her, burned to make this last as long as he could because he was not finishing without her. The power of his words pulsed through her, took her pleasure higher.

Face-to-face, she realized there wasn't a battle for control. They were sharing the moment, sharing the experience. The insight exploded inside her in a shower of light and sensation as she flew apart in his arms. Her cries of completion burst from her in abandon, followed by his. Their voices twined together, echoing out over the ocean.

Panting, she sagged against his chest, perspiration bonding their bodies. Their time together here, away from the rest of the world, had been perfect. Almost too much so.

Now she had to trust in what they'd shared enough to test it out when they returned home.

Seth revved the Cessna seaplane's engines, skimming the craft along the water faster and faster until finally, smoothly...*airborne*.

A few more days on the Outer Banks would have been damn welcome to give him a chance to fortify his connection with Alexa. To experience more of the amazing sex they'd shared in the front seat of the convertible, then the backseat. Except he was out of time.

He had to meet with Pippa tomorrow and hammer

out a new visitation schedule. That always proved sticky since the ugly truth lurked behind every negotiation that he might not be the twins' biological father. If Pippa ever decided to push that, things could go all to hell. He would fight for his kids, but it tore him up inside thinking of how deep it would slice if he lost. Acid burned in his gut.

If only life could be simpler. He just wanted to enjoy his children like any parent. The way his cousin Paige enjoyed hers. The way his cousin Vic was celebrating a new baby with his wife, Claire. That reminded him of what a crappy cousin he'd been in not calling to congratulate them. Paige had texted him that Claire was staying in the hospital longer because of the C-section delivery. He needed to stop by and do the family support gig.

That also meant introducing Alexa to the rest of his family. Soon. His relatives were important to him. He wasn't sure how he was going to piece together his crazy ass life with hers, but walking away wasn't an option. He also wasn't sure how Alexa would feel about his big noisy family, especially given how strained her relationship was with her own.

If only life was as easy to level out as an airplane.

Easing back on the yoke, he scanned his airspeed, along with the rest of the control panel.

Alexa touched the window, an ocean view visible beyond. "I grew up with charter jets, but I've never flown on one of these before. And I certainly didn't have a fleet of planes at my fingertips 24/7."

"This wasn't among my more elite crafts, but, God, I love to fly her."

"I can tell by how relaxed you are here versus other

times." She trapped the toy bobble head fisherman suction-cupped to the control panel. Her finger swayed the line from the fishing pole. "I can hardly believe how much we've done since waking up. Starting in Florida, stopping in South Carolina, North Carolina by lunch. Now home again."

"I still owe you supper, although it'll be late."

"Can we eat it naked?"

"As long as I have you all to myself."

She laughed softly. "While I enjoyed our time in the convertible, I haven't turned into that much of an exhibitionist."

"Good," he growled with more possessiveness than he was used to feeling. "I don't share well."

She toyed with the sleeve of her dress, adjusting it after the haphazard way they'd thrown on their clothes as the sun started to set. "I appreciate that you didn't get weirded out by what I shared with you at the restaurant."

"I admire the way you've taken everything life threw at you and just kept right on kicking back," he answered without hesitation.

He meant every word.

"I'm determined not to let other people steal anything more from me—not my parents or my ex."

"That attitude is exactly what I'm talking about."

"I'm not so sure about the kick-ass thing." Her hand fell to her lap. "It's wacky the way a piece of cheesecake can sometimes still hold me hostage. Sounds strange, I know. I don't expect you to understand."

"Explain it to me." He needed to understand. He couldn't tolerate saying or doing something that could hurt her.

She sagged back in her seat. "Sometimes I look at it

and remember what it was like to want that cheesecake, but then I would measure out how many calories I'd eaten that day. Think how many laps I would need to swim in order to pick up that fork for one bite. Then I would imagine the disappointment on my mother's face when I stepped on the scale the next morning."

What the hell? Her mother made her weigh in every morning? No wonder Alexa had control issues.

He wrestled to keep his face impassive when he really wanted to find her parents and… He didn't know what he would do. He did know he needed to be here for Alexa now. "I wish I'd known you then."

She turned to look at him. "Me, too."

Suddenly he knew exactly where he wanted to take Alexa tonight. "Do you mind staying out late?"

"I'm all for letting this day last as long as possible."

"Good. Then I have one more stop to make on my way to take you home."

Of all the places she thought Seth might take her, Alexa wouldn't have guessed they would go to a hospital.

Once they'd landed, Seth had said he wanted to visit his cousin's new baby. Her heart had leaped to her throat at the mention of an infant. A newborn.

Her skin felt clammy as she rubbed her arms. Was she freaked out because of the baby or because of her own hospital stay? Right now, with her emotions so close to the surface, she couldn't untangle it all.

Damn it, she was being silly. It wasn't like she would even go in to see the new mom. This visit would be over soon and she could clear the antiseptic air with deep breaths outside. Seth was walking in on his own while she hung out at the picture window looking into a nursery packed full of bassinets. Her gaze lingered on one in particular, front row, far left.

Baby Jansen.

She could barely see anything other than a white swaddling blanket and a blue-and-yellow-striped cap. But she could tell the bundle was bigger than most of the others, nearly ten pounds of baby boy, according to Seth. Alexa touched the window lightly, almost imagining she could feel the satiny softness of those chubby newborn cheeks.

A woman stepped up alongside her and Alexa inched to the side to make room.

The blonde woman—in her late thirties—wore a button that proclaimed Proud Aunt. "Beautiful little boy." She tapped the glass right around Baby Jansen territory. "Can you believe all that blond hair? Well, under the hat there's lots of blond hair."

Alexa cocked her head to the side. "Do I know you?"

The woman grinned, and Alexa saw the family resemblance so strongly stamped on her face she might as well have pulled back her question.

"I'm Paige, Seth's cousin. While I was getting coffee, I saw you walking in with him. My brother, Vic, is this baby's daddy."

It was one thing meeting his family with Seth there to handle the introductions, to define their still new relationship. This was awkward to say the least. Why, why, why hadn't she waited in his SUV outside? "Congratulations on your new nephew."

"Thank you, we have lots to celebrate. Hope you'll join us at the next family get-together." She cut her brown eyes toward Alexa. "How did the trip with

Seth and the twins go? They're sweet as can be, but a handful, for sure."

Seth had told his family about her? Curiosity drowned out the rattle of food carts, the echo of televisions, even the occasional squawk of a baby.

"Nice trip. But it's always good to be home," she answered noncommittally. "The twins are back with their mother now."

Paige nodded, tucking her hair behind her ears. "Pippa's, well…" She sighed. "She's Pippa, and she's the twins' mom. And Seth's such a good daddy. He deserves to have a good woman to love him, better than…well…you know."

Sort of. Not really. And she should really cut this short and get all of her answers from Seth. "I'm not in a position to—"

Pivoting, Paige stared her down with an unmistakably protective gleam in her golden-brown eyes. "I'm just asking you to be good to my cousin, to be fair. Pippa screwed him over, literally. There are days I would really like to give her a piece of my mind, but I hold back because I love those kids regardless of whether they're my blood or not. But I don't think I could take seeing him betrayed like that again. So please, if you're not serious, walk away now."

Whoa, whoa, whoa. Alexa struggled to keep up the barrage of information packed into that diatribe. "I don't know what to say other than your family loyalty is admirable?"

"Crap. Sorry." Paige bit her bottom lip. "I should probably hush now. I'm rambling and being rude. Hormones are getting the best of me, compounded even more by the nursery and being pregnant—a whoops, but a happy whoops. And I already get so emotional with how Pippa used Seth, the way she still uses him. I'm sure you're lovely, and I look forward to seeing you again."

Paige squeezed her arm once, before rushing away in a flurry of tissues and winces, leaving Alexa stunned. She looked back into the nursery, then at the departing woman, going over what she'd said, something about whether or not the twins were related to her. And how Pippa had screwed Seth over. Literally.

What the hell? Had Pippa actually cheated on Seth? But he'd said they split before the twins were even born. Not that a pregnant woman couldn't have an affair, but it seemed less likely... Unless... Pippa had the affair while she and Seth were dating, and it only came out later?

An awful possibility smoked through her mind—perhaps the twins weren't his biological children?

She dismissed the thought as quickly as it came to her. He would have shared something like that with her.

Her perceptions of the man jumbled all together. At first, she'd assumed he was like her wealthy parents, too often looking for a way to dump off their kids on the nearest caregiver. Yet, she'd seen with her own eyes how much he loved them, how he spent every free waking moment with them.

If what she suspected was true, why hadn't he said something to her when they'd deepened their relationship? Sure they'd only known each other a short time, but she'd told him everything. He'd insisted on her being open, vulnerable even, when they'd made love by the lighthouse.

Had he been holding back something this important?

She wanted to believe she'd misunderstood Paige. Rather than wonder, she would ask Seth once the timing was right. They would laugh together over how she'd leaped to conclusions. She wanted to trust the feelings growing between her and Seth. More than anything, she wanted this to be real.

And if she was right in her suspicions that he was holding back?

Her eyes skipped to a family at the far end of the picture window. A grandma and grandpa were standing together, shoulder to shoulder, heads tilted toward each other in conversation as they held two older grandchildren up to see their new sister. The connection, the family bond, was undeniable.

She'd seen it earlier today when Seth and Pippa discussed their children. Yes, there was strife between them, but also a certain connection, even tenderness. Disconcerting, regardless. But if they still felt that way after such a betrayal…it gave Alexa pause. It spoke of unresolved feelings between them.

Steadying herself, she pressed her hand to the window. She'd ached for a real family connection growing up, yearned to create such a bond in her marriage. She knew what it felt like to stand on the outside.

And she refused to live that way ever again.

Ten

He wanted Alexa in his life, as well as in his bed.

As Seth drove Alexa home to her downtown Charleston condo after seeing his new nephew, he kept thinking about how right it felt having her sit beside him now. How right it had felt earlier taking her to the hospital with him. Having Alexa with him at such an important family moment made the evening even more special. He hoped when they got to her place, he could persuade her to just pick up some clothes and go with him to his house.

Beams of light from late night traffic streaked through the inky darkness as they crossed the Ashley River. The intimacy of just the two of them in his Infiniti SUV reminded him of making love in the classic Chevy convertible on the Outer Banks. God, was that only a few hours ago? Already, he wanted her again.

And what did she want?

He glanced out of the corner of his eye. She rested her head on the window, cool air from the vent lifting her hair. Shadows played along the dark circles under her eyes, in the furrows along her forehead. He was surprised—and concerned.

"Tell me." He skimmed a strand of hair behind her ear. "What's bothering you?"

She shook her head, keeping her face averted with only the glow of the dashboard lights to help him gauge her mood. She hugged her purse to her chest until the folder inside crackled.

"Whatever it is," he said, "I want to hear it, and don't bother saying it's nothing."

"We're both exhausted." She looked down at her hands, at least not staring out the window but still not turning to him. "It's been an emotional ride since we met, a lot crammed into a short time. I need some space to think."

Crap. She'd asked him earlier if he was giving her the brush-off and now he wondered the same thing. "You're backtracking."

"Maybe."

"Why?" he demanded, considering pulling off the six-lane highway so he could focus his full attention on her.

"Seth, I've worked hard to put my life back together again, twice. As a teenager. And again after my divorce. I'm stronger now because of both of those times. But I still intend to be very careful not to put myself in a dangerous position again."

What the hell? This wasn't the kind of conversation

they should have with him driving. He needed his focus planted firmly on her.

He eyed the fast food restaurant ahead and cut over two lanes of traffic, ignoring the honking horns. He pulled off the interstate and parked under the golden arches.

Hooking his arm on the steering wheel, he pinned her with his gaze. "Let me get this straight. You consider me *dangerous?* What have I done to make you feel threatened?"

"A relationship with you, I mean—" the trenches in her forehead dug deeper "—could be…maybe the better word is chancy." Headlights flashed past, illuminating her face with bright lights in quick, strobelike succession.

Some of the tension melted from his shoulders. His arm slid from the wheel and he took her hand in his. "Any relationship is risky. But I believe we've started something good here."

"I thought so, too, especially this afternoon. I opened up to you in ways I haven't to anyone in as long as I can remember." Her hand was cold in his. "But a relationship has to be a two-way street. Can you deny you're holding back?"

Holding back? Hell, he was giving her more than he'd imagined shelling out after the crap year he'd been through. What more did she want from him? A pint of blood? A pound of flesh?

But snapping those questions at her didn't seem wise. "I'm not sure what you mean."

"You have reservations about us as a couple." She didn't ask. She simply said it.

He couldn't deny she was right on the money.

Now he had to figure out how to work around that in a way that would still involve her packing a sleepover bag to go to his place. "Would it have been better for us to meet a year from now? Absolutely."

"Because?" she pressed.

Damn, he was tired and just wanted to take Alexa to his bed. This wasn't a conversation he wanted to have right now. He didn't much want to have it ever. "A year from now, my divorce wouldn't be as fresh— neither would yours. My kids would be older. Your business would have deeper roots. Can you deny the timing would be better for both of us?"

She shook her head slowly, the air conditioner vent catching the scent of her shampoo. "You know all the reasons why I have issues. I've been completely open with you, and I thought you'd been the same with me."

A buzz started in his brain. She couldn't be hinting at what he thought...

"Your cousin told me about Pippa, how she cheated on you. I can understand why that would make you relationship wary and it would have been helpful to know that."

The buzz in his head increased until he felt like he was being stung by hundreds of bees. Angry bees. Except the rage was his. "Paige had no business telling you that."

"Don't blame her. She thought I already kn—"

"How exactly was I supposed to work that into conversation? Hey, my ex-wife doesn't know for sure if my children are actually mine." His hands fisted. "In fact, she lied to me about that all the way to the altar. Now where would you like to go for dinner?"

Her face paled, her eyes so sympathetic her reaction slashed through all the raw places inside him.

"Seth, I am so sorry."

"I am their father in every way that matters." He slammed his fist into the dash. "I love my kids." His voice cracked.

"I realize that," she said softly, hugging her purse to her stomach.

"It doesn't matter to me whose blood or biology flows through their veins." He thumped his chest right over his heart that he'd placed in two pairs of tiny hands nearly a year ago. "They're *mine*."

"I'm sure they would agree." She paused then continued warily, "Have you taken a paternity test? They certainly look like you."

He didn't need any test to validate his love for those kids. "Back off. This isn't your business."

Her blue eyes filled with tears. "That's my whole point. We may have baggage, but I'm ready to be open about mine. You're not."

"Good God, Alexa, we've barely known each other for a week and you expect me to tell you something that could cripple my kids if they ever found out?"

"You think I would go around telling people? If so, you really don't know me at all." She held up her hands. "You know what? You're one hundred percent correct. This is a mistake. *We* are a mistake. The timing is wrong for us to have a relationship."

The thought of her backing out blindsided him. "Well, there's nothing I can do about the timing."

"My point exactly. Seth, I want to go home now, and I don't want you to follow me inside, and I don't want you to call me."

That was it? Even after their encounter on the Outer Banks, the way they'd come together so magnificently, she was slamming the door in his face? "Damn it, Alexa. Life isn't perfect. I'm not perfect, and I don't expect you to be, either. It's not about all or nothing here."

She chewed her bottom lip and he thought he might be making headway until she looked out the window again without answering.

"What do you want from me, Alexa?"

She turned slowly to him, blue eyes clouded with pain and tears. "Just what I said. I need you to respect my need for space."

Her mouth pursed shut, and she turned her head back toward the window. He waited while four cars cleared the fast food drive-through window and still she wouldn't look at him. He knew an ice-out when he saw one.

Stunned numb, he drove the rest of the way to her condo, a corner unit in a string of red brick buildings made to fit in with the rest of the historic homes. Her place. Where she belonged and he wasn't welcome.

How the hell had it gone so wrong so quickly? So he hadn't told her about Pippa cheating. He would have gotten around to it soon enough.

"Goodbye, Seth." She tore open the door and ran up the walkway into her apartment before he could make it farther than the front of the car.

Frustration chewed his gut as he settled behind the wheel again. He was doing his best here and she was cutting him off at the knees. The way she'd clutched her purse to her chest, she looked like she couldn't get out of the car fast enough. She had probably mangled the folder he'd given her.

An ugly, dark thought snaked through him. That she'd wanted her new contacts and now that she had them, she was looking for a way out. She'd used him. Just as Pippa had used him.

And just that quickly the thought dissipated. He knew Alexa was nothing like Pippa. Sure, they'd come from similar backgrounds, but Alexa had broken free of the dependent lifestyle. She was making her own way in the world. Honestly. With hard work. And she'd been up-front with him from the very start.

If anything, he was the one who'd held back.

Damn it.

She was right.

His head *thunked* against the seat. He'd been carrying so much baggage because of Pippa that he might as well have been driving one of those luggage trucks at the airport. He'd screwed up in that relationship in so many ways and felt the failure all the more acutely in the face of his cousins' marital bliss. To the point that he'd even held back from fully participating in their lives. Sure he'd moved here to be with them, but how close had he let anyone get? How many walls had he built?

None of which was fair to his cousins. And it most definitely wasn't fair to Alexa.

So where did he go from here? Talking to her now would likely only stoke her anger, or worse, stir her tears. Once she had a chance to cool down, he needed to approach her with something more than words. He needed strong actions to show Alexa how special, how irreplaceably important she was to him.

How very much he loved her.

Love.

The word filled his head and settled in with a flawless landing. Damn straight he loved her, and she deserved to know that.

And if she still said no? Then he would work harder. He believed in what they'd shared these past days, in what they'd started to build together.

He hadn't given up in his professional life. Against the odds, regardless of what people told him about waiting until he was older, more established, he'd accomplished what he set out to do.

Now it was time to set his sights on winning over Alexa.

Alexa Randall had accumulated an eclectic box full of lost and found items since opening her own cleaning company for charter jets. There were the standard smart phones, portfolios, tablets, even a Patek Philippe watch. She'd returned each to its owner.

Then there were the stray panties and men's boxers, even the occasional sex toys from Mile High Club members. All of those items, she'd picked up with latex gloves and tossed in the trash.

But the pacifier lying beside a seat reminded her too painfully of the precious twins she'd discovered nearly two weeks ago. Memories of their father pierced her heart all the more.

Her bucket of supplies dropped to the industrial blue carpet with a heavy thud. Ammonia fumes from the rag in her fist stung her eyes. Or maybe it was the tears. Heaven knew, she'd cried more than her fair share since leaving Seth's car after their awful argument a week ago. God, this hurt more than when she'd divorced.

The end of her marriage had been a relief. Losing Seth, however, cut her to the core. So much so, she couldn't escape the fact that she loved him. Truly, deeply loved him.

And he'd let her go.

She'd half expected him to follow her or do something cliché like send bunches of flowers with stock apologies. But he'd done none of that. He'd stayed quiet. Giving her the space she'd demanded? Or walking away altogether?

Her husband and parents would have shouted her down, even going so far as to bully her until she caved.

That made her question how she'd reacted that night to his news about the children. She may have grown in how she stood up for herself since the days when she'd tried to control stress through her eating habits. While she was happy for that newfound strength, perhaps she needed to grow even more to be able to return to a problem and fix it. Real strength wasn't about arguing and stomping away. It was going back to a sticky situation and battling—compromising—for a fair resolution.

And she had no one to blame but herself for condemning him because he hadn't told her all his secrets right away. How fair had that been?

Yes, he'd held back. Yet to the best of his ability, he'd lived up to everything he'd promised, everything he was able to give right now. Why was she realizing this now rather than days ago when she could have saved herself so much pain?

Most likely because she'd hidden her head in the sand the past few days, crying her eyes out and burying herself in paperwork at the office. Today was her first day actually picking up a bucket—and what a day it was with so many reminders of Seth and his kids.

She looked around the private luxury jet owned by Senator Landis, parked at the Charleston airport—not Seth's private field. But still, with that pacifier in hand from one of the Landis babies, she couldn't help but think of Owen and Olivia, and wonder how they were doing. She'd missed their sweet faces this week as well, and she liked to think they'd felt a connection to her, too, even during their short time together.

Her ultimatum had hurt more than just her. She stared into the bucket, more of those tears springing to her eyes. Blaming them on ammonia wouldn't work indefinitely.

She sank down onto the leather sofa, her mind replaying for the millionth time the harsh words they'd shared. She looked around the pristinely clean aircraft and wished her life was as easy to perfect.

Perfect?

Her mind snagged on the word, shuffling back to something Seth had said about it not being the perfect time, but life wasn't perfect. He didn't expect her to be perfect… And… What? She reached for the thought like an elusive pristine cloud until—

An increasing ruckus outside broke her train of thought. The sound of trucks and people talking in a rising excited cacophony of voices. She stood and walked toward the hatch. Bits of conversation drifted toward her.

"What's that up—?"

"—airplane?"

"P-47 Thunderbolt, I th—"

"Can you read what—?"

"—wonder who is Alexa?"

Alexa? Airplane?

A hope too scary to acknowledge prickled along her skin. She stepped into the open hatch, stopping at the top of the metal stairs. Shading her eyes, she scanned the crowd of maintenance workers and aircraft service personnel. She followed the path of their fingers pointing upward.

A World War II-era plane buzzed low over their section of the airfield, a craft that looked remarkably like the one she'd seen in Seth's hangar. Trailing behind, a banner flapped against the bright blue sky. In block red letters, it spelled out:

I Love You, Alexa Randall!

Her breath hitched in her throat as she descended the steps one at a time, rereading the message. By the time her feet hit concrete, it had fully sunk in. Seth was making a grand gesture to win her back. Her. Alexa Randall. At an imperfect time. In spite of her frustrated fears that were far from rational.

She'd thought she'd left her growing up years behind her, but she'd been hanging on to more than a need to make the world around her perfectly in order. She'd still subconsciously held onto the old, misguided mantra that *she* had to be perfect as well.

Seth had told her that didn't matter to him.

Maybe she needed to remember Seth didn't need to be perfect, either.

And she couldn't wait for him to land so she could tell him face-to-face.

The plane circled once more, message rippling for the entire airport to see. Then the craft descended, drifting downward into a smooth landing only twenty feet away from her.

The engine shut off with a rattle. The whirring rotor on the nose slowed and finally *click, click, clicked* to a stop. And there he was. *Seth.* Big, blond, bold and all *hers.*

He jumped out of the old craft, wearing khakis, hiking boots and a loose white shirt. His broad shoulders blocked out the sun and the crowd. Or maybe that was just because when he walked into her world, everything else went fuzzy around the edges.

She threw away the rag in her hand and raced toward him. A smile stretched across his face, his arms opening just as wide. She flew into his embrace, soaking up the crisp, clean scent of him.

She kissed him. Right there in front of the cheering crowd of airport personnel as he spun her around. The other voices and applause growing dimmer in her ears, she lost herself in the moment and just held tight to Seth. Even after her feet touched ground again, her head still twirled.

Moisture burned behind her eyelids, the happy kind of tears. How amazing to find her perfect love in accepting their imperfections.

He whispered in her ear. "Now maybe we can take this conversation somewhere a bit more private."

"I happen to be cleaning that plane right behind you and no one's due to show up for at least a half hour."

He scooped her into his arms—which launched another round of applause from the crowd—and he jogged up the steps, turning sideways to duck into the plane. He set her on her feet and right back into his arms.

Holding him closer, she laughed into his neck, his shirt warm against her cheek. "How did you know I was here?"

"I had an inside track on your work schedules. Senator Landis is a cousin of mine, sort of, with his wife being the foster sister of my cousin's wife... My family. There are a lot of us." He guided her to the leather sofa. "Before we talk about anything else, I need to tell you a few things."

Good or bad? She couldn't tell from the serious set of his face. "Okay, I'm listening."

"I've spent the past week working out some new custody arrangements with Pippa. The twins will be spending more time with me, and we've hired a new nanny for when they're with her." He looked down at their joined hands, his fingers twitching. "I'm not ready to run that paternity test. I don't know if I ever will be. The other guy who could be their biological father doesn't want anything to do with them. So, I want to leave things as they are for now. I just want to enjoy watching my kids grow up."

"I can understand that." She wanted that same joy in her life. The way he loved the twins made total sense to her. She'd been completely certain she would love an adopted child during her first marriage. "I'm sorry for pushing you away."

His knuckle glided gently along her cheekbone. "And I'm sorry for not being more open with you."

She cradled his face in her hands. "I can't believe the way you flew out there. You're crazy, did you know that?"

"When it comes to you, yes I am." He pressed a

lingering kiss into her palm, before pointing a thumb toward his airplane outside. "Did you get my message?"

"There wasn't any missing it." She tipped her face to his.

"I meant it, every word." His emerald eyes glinting with a gemstone radiance and strength. "I should have said them to you that night. Even before that. I was so zeroed in on my need to keep my kids' lives stable I focused on the idea of making sure they didn't have a parade of women through their lives. I almost missed the bigger message knocking around in my brain."

Her arms around his neck, she toyed with his sun-kissed hair. "And that message would be?"

"Marry me, Alexa." He pressed a hand to her lips, his fingertips callused. "I realize this is moving too fast in some ways and in other ways I haven't moved quickly enough. But if you need to wait a while, I can be patient. You're worth it."

"I know," she said confidently, realizing for maybe the first time she did deserve this man and his love. They both deserved to be happy together. "And I love you, too. The bold way that you touch me and challenge me. How tenderly you care for your children. You are everything I could want, everything I never even knew I could have."

"I love you, Alexa." He stroked her hair back from her face. "You. The beautiful way you are with my kids. The way you try to take care of everyone around you. But I also want to be here to take care of you when you demand too much of yourself. I love the perfect parts of us being together—and even the parts of us that aren't perfect but somehow fit together. Bottom line, you have to trust me when I say I love you and I want to be with you for the rest of my life."

"Starting now," she agreed.

"Starting right this second, if you're done here."

She scooped up her bucket. "As a matter of fact, I am. What did you have in mind?

"A date, an honest to God, going out to dinner together date—" he punctuated each plan with a kiss "—followed by more dates and making out and sex—lots of sex—followed by more romancing your socks off."

She sighed against his mouth, swaying closer to him. "And we get married."

"Yes, ma'am," he promised, "and then the real romancing begins."

Epilogue

A year later

She couldn't have asked for a more romantic wedding.

And it had nothing to do with pomp and circumstance. In fact she and Seth had bypassed all of that and planned a beach wedding in Charleston that focused on family. A very *large* family, all in attendance.

Her bouquet in one hand, Alexa looped her other arm around her husband's neck and lost herself in the toe-tingling beauty of their first kiss as man and wife. Her skin warmed from the late day sun and the promise of their honeymoon in the outer banks—of Greece.

The kiss still shimmering to the roots of her upswept hair, Alexa eased back down to her toes. Applause and cheers echoed with the rustle of sea oats. She scooped up Olivia and Seth hefted up Owen. Arm in arm with her husband, she turned to face the hundred guests. Waves rolled and crashed in time with the steel drums playing as they walked back down the aisle lined with lilies and palm fronds. The sun's rays glittered off the sand and water like billions of diamonds had been ordered special for the day.

The twins, now nearly two and nonstop chatter bugs, clapped along with the guests. Shortly before the wedding, Seth had quietly seen the doctor about running a paternity test. As Alexa had suspected all along, the babies were Seth's biological children. His relief had been enormous. He'd credited her love with giving him the strength to take that step.

A love they were celebrating today.

Sand swirled around her ankles, the perfume of her bouquet swelling upward—a mix of calla lilies, orchids and roses, with trailing stephanotis. The attire had been kept casual, with pink flowing sundresses for both bridesmaids. For the men, khakis with white shirts— and rose boutonnieres that had arrived in the *wrong* color. But she knew it was a sign that they were ideal for her wedding because the deep crimson rose was a lovely wink and nod to the beauty of the imperfect.

And her dress… White organza flowed straight down from the fitted bodice with diamond spaghetti straps. No heels to get caught in the sand, just bare feet, miles of pristine beach and crystal blue waters. A very familiar and dear World War II vintage aircraft flew overhead carrying a banner for the entire wedding party to see.

Congratulations, Mr. and Mrs. Seth Jansen.

Cabanas with dining tables filled the beach, complete with a large tent and jazz band for dancing later. She'd let her new caterer-cousin choose the menu and design a detailed sandcastle wedding cake fit for a princess. And ironically enough, she had an entire Medina royal family in attendance as well as the Landises, considered by some to be American political royalty.

A play area with babysitters on hand had been roped off for children with their own special menu and cupcakes with crystallized sugar seashells on top. Although already kids were playing outside the designated area carefully arranged for them. They were happily building a sandcastle town with new moms Paige and Claire overseeing them. Just the way it should be—with everyone enjoying the day.

She and Seth had wanted their wedding to celebrate family, and they'd succeeded. Even her family was in attendance. While their relationship would likely never be close, enjoying a peaceful visit with them went a long way in soothing old hurts.

She and Seth had spent the past year building their relationship, strengthening the connection they'd felt so tangibly from the start. She'd also spent the past twelve months building her business and confidence. Her favorite work? Servicing the search and rescue planes on the philanthropic side of Jansen Jets. It was not the whole company, but certainly the part most near and dear to Seth's heart.

They were both living out their dreams.

She looked from their applauding relatives to her new husband. And what do you know?

He was already staring right back at her, his eyes full of love. "Is everything turning out the way you wanted today?"

She toyed with his off-color rose boutonniere. "The day couldn't be any more perfect."

And the best part of that? She knew each of their tomorrows promised to be even better.

* * * * *

Harlequin Desire

COMING NEXT MONTH

Available November 8, 2011

*Harlequin® Special Edition® is thrilled to present a new
installment in USA TODAY bestselling author
RaeAnne Thayne's reader-favorite miniseries,
THE COWBOYS OF COLD CREEK.*

*Join the excitement as we meet the Bowmans—four
siblings who lost their parents but keep family ties alive
in Pine Gulch. First up is Trace. Only two things get under
this rugged lawman's skin: beautiful women and secrets.
And in Rebecca Parsons, he finds both!*

*Read on for a sneak peek of
CHRISTMAS IN COLD CREEK.
Available November 2011 from Harlequin® Special Edition®.*

On impulse, he unfolded himself from the bar stool. "Need
a hand?"

"Thank you! I…" She lifted her gaze from the floor to
his jeans and then raised her eyes. When she identified him
her hazel eyes turned from grateful to unfriendly and cold,
as if he'd somehow thrown the broken glasses at her head.

He also thought he saw a glimmer of panic in those
interesting depths, which instantly stirred his curiosity like
cream swirling through coffee.

"I've got it, Officer. Thank you." Her voice was several
degrees colder than the whirl of sleet outside the windows.

Despite her protests, he knelt down beside her and began
to pick up shards of broken glass. "No problem. Those trays
can be slippery."

This close, he picked up the scent of her, something fresh
and flowery that made him think of a mountain meadow on
a July afternoon. She had a soft, lush mouth and for one
brief, insane moment, he wanted to push aside that stray lock

of hair slipping from her ponytail and taste her. Apparently he needed to spend a lot less time working and a great deal *more* time recreating with the opposite sex if he could have sudden random fantasies about a woman he wasn't even inclined to like, pretty or not.

"I'm Trace Bowman. You must be new in town."

She didn't answer immediately and he could almost see the wheels turning in her head. Why the hesitancy? And why that little hint of unease he could see clouding the edge of her gaze? His presence was obviously making her uncomfortable and Trace couldn't help wondering why.

"Yes. We've been here a few weeks."

"Well, I'm just up the road about four lots, in the white house with the cedar shake roof, if you or your daughter need anything." He smiled at her as he picked up the last shard of glass and set it on her tray.

Definitely a story there, he thought as she hurried away. He just might need to dig a little into her background to find out why someone with fine clothes and nice jewelry, and who so obviously didn't have experience as a waitress, would be here slinging hash at The Gulch. Was she running away from someone? A bad marriage?

So…Rebecca Parsons. Not Becky. An intriguing woman. It had been a long time since one of those had crossed his path here in Pine Gulch.

Trace won't rest until he finds out Rebecca's secret, but will he still have that same attraction to her once he does? Find out in CHRISTMAS IN COLD CREEK. Available November 2011 from Harlequin® Special Edition®.

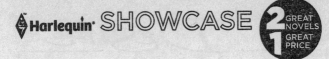

Discover two classic tales of romance in one
incredible volume from

USA TODAY **Bestselling Author**

Catherine
Mann

Two powerful, passionate men
are determined to win back the women
who haunt their dreams...but it will
take more than just seduction
to convince them that this love will last.

IRRESISTIBLY HIS

Available October 25, 2011.

Harlequin *Presents*®

brings you

USA TODAY Bestselling Author

Penny Jordan

Part of the new miniseries

***Demidov vs. Androvonov—let the most
merciless of men win...***

Kiryl Androvonov
The Russian oligarch has one rival: billionaire
Vasilii Demidov. Luckily, Vasilii has an Achilles' heel—his
younger, overprotected, beautiful half sister, Alena...

Vasilii Demidov
After losing his sister to his bitter rival, Vasilii is far too
cynical to ever trust a woman, not even his secretary Laura.
Never did she expect to be at the ruthless Russian's mercy....

The rivalry begins in...

THE MOST COVETED PRIZE—November
THE POWER OF VASILII—December

Available wherever
Harlequin Presents® books are sold.

www.Harlequin.com

HP13023

Harlequin®

ROMANTIC

SUSPENSE

CARLA CASSIDY

Cowboy's Triplet Trouble

Jake Johnson, the eldest of his triplet brothers, is stunned
when Grace Sinclair turns up on his family's ranch declaring
Jake's younger and irresponsible brother as the father of her
triplets. When Grace's life is threatened, Jake finds himself
fighting a powerful attraction and a need to protect. But as
the threats hit closer to home, Jake begins to wonder
if someone on the ranch is out to kill Grace....

A brand-new Top Secret Deliveries story!

TOP SECRET
DELIVERIES

Available in November wherever books are sold!